The six men stiffened into line, short carbines tight against right legs. They faced a section of the dun-colored wall, and the stubby stained post planted solidly before it. In response to Sergeant Charlie Ward's command the firing squad turned half-right to the wall and brought pieces smoothly to the ready. Six eyes squinted along six cold gun barrels at the mute and bullet-pocked post.

"Cock your locks!"

Dry snicks in unison.

"Take your aim . . ."

Ward's sabre raised and he measured the squad, preparing to bring the blade sweeping down in the command to fire. The troopers tensed. But the sabre didn't fall. The Sergeant was staring, eyes wide and fixed, at a deeply embrasured window of the guardhouse. There was a face in the window. A white smear in deep shadow. A film of perspiration broke on Ward's upper lip. The man in the window was Fargo. He was watching them practice for his own death.

Fawcett Gold Medal Books
by E. M. Parsons:

THE EASY GUN

FARGO

FARGO

E. M. Parsons

A Fawcett Gold Medal Book
Fawcett Publications, Inc., Greenwich, Conn.

All characters in this book are fictional, and any resemblance to persons living or dead is purely coincidental.

© 1968 CBS Publications, The Consumer Publishing Division of CBS, Inc. All Rights Reserved.

Printed in the United States of America

FARGO

Chapter 1

THE MULES HAD stopped. There were six of them, big and rangy animals wearing outsize U.S.A. brands, hitched to a sutler's box-bodied wagon. They had pulled it all night, racing the dawn toward the mountains just now becoming visible to the west. A knife wind tumbled dry balls of weed and brought a sharp smell of snow. Heartbreak country. Scattered clumps of buffalo grass pushing up through hardpan swept perpetually by keening winds. No roads, no houses, no rising smoke in all that crackling emptiness.

A wagon, six mules and a man.

Fargo knew the wagon had stopped. Through the deep comfort of exhausted sleep something prodded. There was some reason why stopping was bad. He slumped motionless on the wagon's hard seat, reins dangling limply from one wind-reddened hand. He was a big man even huddled as he was. Big shoulders, big hands—face strong and unruly, no slack even in sleep.

The off-wheeler snorted and stomped, harness jangling. Fargo came awake all at once. He straightened and a jab of pain hit him high up on the right side. It all came back, then, rushing into his awareness. Charlie Ward! The firing squad and Charlie Ward and the wild stampede through the Dakota night. He swiveled to look at his back trail. It was full light now to the east. He surveyed the horizon with method and thoroughness, from point to point along the skyline—like a soldier. There was a warm trickle from his armpit, down his side. Damn Henry made a hole a man could carry his lunch in. His right hand was numb, the arm useless. He shoved his hand between buttons on the coat—a rough sling. Later, he'd strap it up if he got time.

"Hah." His breath hissed out with the soft exclamation, puffing white and wispy. "There's old Charlie . . ."

Far back against a slight dip in the eastern horizon a thin haze sharpened in the cold sky, dust hanging high. Could be a wandering band of Blackfeet, maybe, or Sioux. But it wasn't; he knew it wasn't. It was Charlie Ward with a troop from Fort Denman and they were after him.

He was stiff from the cold ride and the aftermath of physical violence. But he had to move. The hole in his back didn't help though he ignored it, knowing he had to. The wagon had been almost unloaded when he rode it out of the fort the night before. Only one bale remained in the bed and Fargo dumped it over the tailgate, hoping it contained something that would help him face the trail ahead. The bale split when it hit the ground scattering clanging metal on the hardpan. Mess kits. Mess kits and bayonets.

His face tightened a little and he lifted his gaze to the dust plume, a dark smudge now, hanging high and getting closer. Thin and high, that smudge. A half-troop, probably. And riding tired horses after the all night chase. He turned to look toward the low-lying mountains ahead. There'd be snow up there. And safety—for a man strong enough and lucky enough.

He shrugged. There was no real choice. After four years of war, three times sergeant and four times wounded and all the time sickened by the useless killing, he'd developed a talent for survival. He would need all of that talent now.

Clumsy with only one hand, he picked a mess kit out of the scrabble and stuffed it in a jacket pocket. He shoved a new bayonet through his belt next to Charlie's Navy Colt. Then he got another bayonet, flipped away the scabbard and walked around to the mules. The army blade glittered and hissed, chopping traces, straps, hames. A final slash and the doubletree fell away. The mule hitch was free of the wagon but the mules were still hooked to each other. He rolled the long supple reins as he walked to the lead mules. Later, he'd cut the lines to a more manageable length but right now he was running out of time.

He looked back. Coming pretty steady for tired horses, he thought. A half-troop, all right. And though it was much too far to distinguish single riders, the burn in his belly let him imagine Charlie Ward riding in the van.

"Better hope you don't catch me, Charlie," he muttered.

He grabbed a handful of harness and mane, hoisted himself aboard the tall off-leader. The mule danced, stirring the whole hitch. Fargo took a tight hold on the mass of reins and kicked hard with both heels.

"Heeyah! Get outa that!"

The mules jumped into ragged motion. Fargo whooped and dug his heels into the startled animal again. The hitch flattened out to a dead run across the level plain, running rough then smoothing out to perfect unison, ears laid back and haunches bunching rhythmically, driven by the wildly yelling man and pulling only the wind. . . .

The cavalry detail straggled up to the wagon at a dead-legged trot. The noncom in the lead was a stocky, red-faced man with ginger side-whiskers and a bloody rag slanted around his head. His eyes appeared colorless in the unrelenting morning light. He sat his jaded mount, pale eyes flitting, touching the wagon, the cut harness the jumble of mess kits. The others sat with that apathetic withdrawn look of tired men, totally disinterested. The horses stood hipshot, heads drooping.

"Looks like ol' Fargo's long gone, Sar'nt," a young trooper offered, not caring one way or the other.

Sergeant Ward glanced at the kid and there was

more emotion in the look than the remark seemed to warrant. A sharp-faced veteran with dark marks on his sleeves where chevrons had been once, urged his mount up beside the noncom. He spoke without looking at the other.

"He cut the whole hitch loose. Ridin' one at a time, cut 'em out of the hitch when they founder. Gonna be hard to catch, Charlie."

"We'll catch him." Ward's voice was rusty, like iron. He nudged his animal close to the driver's box, reached out a gauntleted hand. "Look here. Blood. He's hurt."

The young trooper cursed with small spirit. "So he's hurt. How come you to be so set on taking him back to be shot, anyway? He's your friend, ain't he?"

Ward's gaze hardened. "He's a deserter."

"War's over, Charlie." It was the veteran, his soft voice carefully lacking feeling. "Sergeant Fargo come a long way with us. You and me. Manassas—Valparaiso and Malvern, Shitty Junction. . . ."

"*Not* Sergeant Fargo. General Prisoner Fargo." Ward kept his gaze on the purpling hills to the west. "I'm going after him. Y'all do what you want to."

His hand came up and touched the crusted bandage on his head. He pulled his horse around, not looking at the men of his detail. Then he kicked the weary animal into motion, lifted it into a stumbling trot toward those distant mountains.

The young one said, "Good jumpin' goddam. Virg, these hides won't last til' noon."

The veteran trooper nodded, agreeing. "What gravels me is why."

"Yeah. Why is ol' Ward so hot after Fargo? He got his stripes and now looks like he wants his ass, too."

Another trooper spoke. "I say let's get on back to Denman. I'm tired and cold and don't need no more pounding on this damned bonerack."

"Me too," the kid agreed. "Sergeant Ward he said

we could do what we want to, Virg. What do you think? I don't want to see ol' Fargo shot, noway."

The veteran gathered his reins. "I know what he said, Denzel. But we're still in the army and he's in charge of this detail. Let's go." He pulled his mount around, then paused, turning to the young trooper. "Don't be worrying too much about Sergeant Fargo. He takes a lot of killing."

The half-troop creaked into motion, tired men and tired horses, clattering over an alien land, pursuing a vengeance none of them understood.

Charlie Ward understood. He understood in his belly if not in his head. He rode unfeeling to the racking and exhausted the trot of his horse. Had the animal fallen under him, Charlie would have felt only a brief irritation before beginning to walk toward those hills. After Fargo.

"Goddam Fargo! Damn him to hell!"

Yesterday. Only twenty-four hours yet the whole world turned with a different rhythm. Nothing was the same or would ever be again. How could a man lose his hold on life in only twenty-four hours?

It had started with the firing squad drill. Denman was a cold post standing as it did smack in the middle of nothing at all, protecting nothing and—so most of the bitter veterans said—worth nothing. And the wind seemed colder than usual to the squad lined up near the guardhouse. Maybe because of what they were doing. It was dusk and the flagstaff stood naked. Debris rolled across the quad and sentries were headhunched, cursing. Sergeant Ward stood to one side of the six-man detail and his rusty voice was rasping in the chill.

"We can stay out here all night if you want to. What the hell you think this is—fun? Something I made up as a goddam joke?"

It had been the kid. Again. He was squirming under Ward's words, holding out gloveless hands.

"It's cold, Sar'nt. Cripes, my fingers feels like froze carrots."

"You'll get warm walkin' quad tonight in full field 'n fodder if I don't hear that sling pop this time! You hear me, Denzel? Pop!" He slapped his boot with the naked saber he held. "All right—once like it ought to be. Ten-*hut!*"

The six men stiffened into line, short carbines tight against right legs. They faced a blank section of the dun-colored wall, blank except for the stubby, stained post planted solidly in the ground before it. In response to Ward's crisp commands, the firing squad turned half-right to the wall and brought pieces smoothly to the ready. Six eyes squinted along six cold gun-barrels at the mute and bullet-pocked post.

"Cock your locks!"

Dry snicks in unison.

"Take your aim. . . ."

Ward's saber raised and he measured the squad in readiness to bring the blade sweeping down in the command to fire. The troopers tensed. But the saber did not fall. The sergeant was staring, eyes wide and fixed, at a deep-embrasured window of the guard-house. There was a face in the window. A white blob in deep shadow. A film of perspiration broke on Ward's upper lip despite the cold. The men stirred, began to mutter.

"Recover," Ward husked. He let the saber down slowly. "Too cold to practice. Dismissed!"

The men broke up and dispersed, hurrying for the dubious warmth of the barracks. A pinch-faced trooper spoke to Ward, got no answer. Then, noting the direction of the noncom's fixed gaze, he shrugged and straggled after the others.

A mule hitch pulled a loaded wagon through the open front gate and wheeled it into position for unloading in front of the sutler's. Lights came on here and there. A lieutenant with a guardsman's mustache trotted out of HQ and started across the quadrangle, stepping briskly. He passed Ward.

"Come with me, Sergeant."

Not waiting for Ward's automatic "Yessir," he continued purposefully to the low, log building which housed the fort's occasional offenders. The sentry at the door came to attention, snapping his Henry to the salute. The officer pulled open the heavy outside door and entered. Ward lingered in the open door.

"Go get some coffee," he muttered to the chilled sentry. "Warm up. I'll be here."

The man nodded gratefully, started away.

"Leave the rifle. I'll take care of it."

Inside, the wind sound was muted. The lieutenant waited impatiently by a door at the far end of the narrow corridor. Ward put the sentry's rifle in a corner near the door and hurried to join the officer.

There was only one cell in the section they entered; and only one man in it, standing with his back to the door. He heard them enter but he didn't turn. His big-knuckled hands gripped thick bars in a chest-high window which had inside shutters folded open against the wall. Cold wind ruffled the man's dark hair and chilled the already austere interior.

"Fargo."

The lieutenant stopped before the cell door. Ward stopped a pace to the rear and beside him, stiff and military. The officer pulled a sheaf of papers from his gauntlet.

"Come away from that window, man," he said. He rattled his papers. "Look here, now—I've got to deliver these charges and specifications to the accused. Them's the rules."

For a long moment, Fargo did not move and the silence thickened and stretched. Ward thought he heard a sigh and the prisoner moved, unclamping his fingers deliberately from the bars. Then, he gently closed the shutters against the seeking wind and turned. His eyes were very dark and sharp, finding Ward and holding on him.

"Soldier," the officer said, "these are proceedings for the general court, wherein you are charged with conduct 'prejudicial to good order and military discipline.' That's charge one. Article ninety-three, 'general orders'."

He snapped the stiff paper, gnawed at his mustache. He seemed to have no liking for the chore. His rather bulbous eyes lifted up to the prisoner.

"Supposed to read 'em to you. Specifications and all. That's the rule." He creased the sheaf and stuffed it between the bars. "Hell, you know what it says. Here. . . ."

Fargo took the papers, his gaze never leaving Charlie Ward. His strong fingers smoothed the sheets absently. The Lieutenant slapped a glove loudly.

"Damn! Look here—I'll be there tomorrow. Do what I can." He turned almost angrily on Ward. "Sergeant! See this man gets a shave and clean uniform. You hear?"

"Yessir!" Ward saluted and the officer left, almost running, bootheels rapping in the corridor. The outside door banged and there was nothing left but the silence and two men—and the grim image of a stained post, waiting.

"They're fixing to kill me, Charlie."

"You don't know that, Fargo. You ain't been tried yet. Anything can happen." The words tumbled out in a rush, expressing his relief at having this out and done with. "The war's over. You're a good soldier. They ain't gonna shoot a man as good as you. They—"

He stopped. Fargo just looked at him.

Ward said, "You *did* run! They caught you."

"Sure, I ran." Fargo's voice was soft. "You ran too, Charlie. We all did."

Charlie's hand went to the Navy Colt at his belt and he took a quick step forward.

"Don't say that! Nobody run but you!"

Fargo's lips twisted; his eyes held Ward's and they were steady and clear. Charlie looked away.

"What good is all that, now. What *good* is it? You got caught—only you. That's all that matters."

The big man moved to the bars in one lithe step and Ward jumped back despite himself. "You bet that's all that matters," he said. His voice got thick. "They're going to tie me to that old post out there and my friend drops his saber and Fargo's dead! Dead by the numbers—hup, two, three. Murder by the goddam numbers and nobody cares!"

Ward looked fearfully at the door. "Be quiet! You crazy hollering like that. Anybody might hear."

"Let 'em. You hear, too, Charlie. Hear good. I wore out this dirty damn war and I stayed alive and I'm not dying now! Not for you—not for nobody. I'm gonna talk loud and clear tomorrow, Charlie. Loud and clear."

The threat was clear to Ward and he felt fear, cold and thrusting. He pulled the ring of guardhouse keys from his belt.

"Listen," he said, voice firm again. "I'm supposed to get you cleaned up—shaved. . . ." He fumbled a key into the lock, swung the cell door wide. "It was an order, wasn't it? I'll say you jumped me, hit me with something."

Fargo did not move. "There's a guard outside."

"I sent him away. Come on, man! It's all I can do. Get out of there!"

Hope and purpose flickered in Fargo's eyes but he did not step through the door. "You got a gun there, Charlie."

"Gawdalmighty—here!" He ripped the Colt free of its holster, flipped it toward Fargo. *"Will you git!"*

Fargo plucked the gun smoothly out of the air and came alive. He jumped past Ward, jerking open the door to the corridor. Then he stopped abruptly, turned.

"I thought bad about you, Charlie. I'm glad I was wrong."

Then he was gone.

Ward listened for the small sound of the front door being eased closed before he moved. When it came he quickly rumpled his uniform, knocked off his forage cap and stepped on it. The cell door was all bars and very heavy. He swung it back and forth. It moved easily on oiled hinges. He pushed it closed, stood in front of it as a man would in the act of opening it. Then he yanked the door with all his strength and braced him self in the path of the swinging mass of iron, closing his eyes.

The door crashed into him hard. It drove him to his knees. His head was cut and that was his blood dripping to the floor. For a moment he was stunned. But his hard purpose pulled him up and out the corridor. The Henry was still there in the deep shadow beside the entrance. He picked it up, cracked the door and peered out through the slitted opening.

It was deep dark now. The Post quadrangle was all but devoid of movement. The wagon and team stood at the sutler's porch while a bulky teamster in shirt sleeves moved back and forth emptying it. A lone sentry huddled to one side of the open gate, greatcoat turned up against the wind. The gate. That's what Fargo had to reach; there was no other way out of the small fort. Ward's exposed eye watered in the freezing wind as he searched for Fargo—a telltale bulk of dark shadow. He saw it. By the farrier's hut. The figure was crouched and obviously intent on the unloading activity at the sutler's. He did not see Ward.

Ward's gaze searched the quad looking for possible cover for Fargo when he broke. There was none. The square was bare except for the saluting cannon with its tiny pyramid of shot next to the flagstaff. No cover for anyone trying to get to the gate. None at all.

Ward waited.

Fargo waited, too. Until the teamster, cursing in a

loud brogue at someone inside the open door of the store, shouldered a load and disappeared with it. Then Fargo moved all at once and straight at his objective, running with a crouched stride, head swiveling.

"Damn him, he's a soldier," Ward muttered. "The sonofabitch is a soldier. Now!"

The last word was shouted and with it he kicked open the door, stepping out into the wind-whipped quad. He racked a load into the Henry, lifted it. Fargo was in the middle of the open square with no place in the world to go. He was alone, running. Ward fired, leading him a little and Fargo slammed to the ground as the heavy slug hit him. Quick triumph choked Charlie and he aimed for a finishing shot. A film of blood from his head wound ran into his eye blinding him. He cursed, thumbed his eyes.

"Corp'rl the guard! Post number one!" He fired blindly.

When his vision cleared, he saw the ball burn dirt near the downed man's head. Fargo rolled like a weasel, squirmed for the only thing in sight—the stack of iron shot for the saluting cannon. And he got there. Charlie cracked a shot off the iron and it whined spitefully into the night.

A spurt of orange fire lanced out from behind the pyramid of shot. Fargo was shooting at the mule team! He fired again and the animals jumped and pulled, eyes rolling. Ward squeezed off another shot with no hope of hitting the fugitive. He looked around for the guard detail. Where the hell was everyone? Only the sentry at the gate had moved, planting himself solidly in the opening. But he had no idea what was going on or who to shoot at.

Fargo fired again and the mules went into a frenzy, pulled away from the clutching hands of the teamster and took off across the quad, the wagon rumbling behind.

"Watch the gate!" Ward shouted. He raised the Henry and fired until the piece was empty, cursing as the crazed mules pounded across the square at the only opening they could see—the wide open main gate.

It was a beautiful move Fargo made. It would have been impressive for a healthy man; for one with a fifty-grain bullet in his upper back it was miraculous. The flying mules were in a wild-eyed gallop passing the flagstaff when Fargo, timing his sprint perfectly, caught the rear corner of the wagon box on the dead run as it flashed by. Then he was bounding along in great leaps pulled by the stampeding animals in their headlong run.

The gate sentry dove to the ground at the last moment to avoid being run down. Ward sprinted to the gate, but the wagon was gone, tearing away downslope dragging Fargo behind. Ward saw him trying to reach the top of the tailgate with the hand on his wounded side, but the hand would not grip. He held on grimly with one, his body twisting and turning with the drag of his feet on the ground.

Once, when his head turned back, Ward saw a flash of white in the dark, a straining face, and he could have sworn he heard Fargo laugh. . .

Chapter 2

FARGO KILLED THE last mule three days after the run from the prairie. The animal had stumbled in the drifting snow and kneeled forward, exhausted. Fargo, hollow-eyed and whiskered, with a webbing of harness and reins wrapped around his upper body, pulled himself out of the drift where the mule's fall had dumped him.

The mule was done. Finished. No doubt about that at all. Its head was buried in the snow, hindquarters elevated, gaunt flanks heaved, but the mule was all through.

Fargo carefully pushed himself up. He wavered, weak from loss of blood and no food. No food except a few strips of mule liver and there was damn little nourishment in that. He moved to the foundered animal unsheathing his bayonet on the way. He touched the blade to the beast's throat; there was a pulse but only just. . . . While the mule was alive he had company. Something living. He needed food more than company so he cut the mule's throat.

It took him until daylight the next morning to skin one haunch and disjoint it. He worked in a half-stupor, not feeling the cold. When he fell, as he did repeatedly, cold snow on his face brought him around——or the dull pain in his back and shoulder.

The dawn was slate and chilly, holding promise of bad weather. Fargo peered at the eastern horizon through slit lids. Another storm. Maybe a big one. He wondered idly if this was the one that would kill him.

"No!" His own voice startled him in the mountain quiet. "Not gonna die, Charlie. Not."

He found a boulder to prop himself up since he didn't dare sit down. Better take inventory. Have to find some place to ride out the storm. If it caught him in the open he would freeze. He had the Colt and two shells for it. Mess cup and bayonet. Several yards of harness leather and a quarter of raw mule, too heavy to carry. Not bad. Enough, maybe. A grin touched his stiff lips. It would have to be enough.

He pushed off from the rock, marked the spot in his mind. Up—he'd go up. Find some sort of cave, maybe, or a place in the rocks to build a shelter. He went up, his legs pushing unfeelingly through the snow. The wind grew louder and stronger bringing the first sharp spatters of snow.

What he found wasn't a cave at all. Just a place where a tall slab-rock tilted against the bottom of a small cliff. But it was the only shelter he'd seen. He had come less than a quarter-mile but already the thickening flurries hampered movement. Couldn't see twenty feet straight ahead. Time to go to earth. The opening of the shelter was narrow and diminished toward the top. Fargo got down on his knees and peered inside. It was dry. Without a fire though, he'd still freeze. He looked back out at the storm, at the canyon he'd just come up stretching into dancing white infinity. This would have to be it.

He threw his stuff inside. The Colt, mess cup, most of the clinging harness, and the mule liver, now frozen. He kept his bayonet and about twenty feet of the limber reins. If he found some burnable wood he'd have to drag it back somehow. The mean little shelter was inviting; he knew, though, if he crawled into the calm even for a short rest he would never get his abused body moving again.

He lurched up, started toward what looked like a small clump of trees. If he could find them through the snow and find his way back. Snow stung his eyes and got into his mouth. He lowered his head and kept moving. Don't worry, Charlie, Fargo ain't done yet. Not quite yet. He leaned into the treacherous wind and concentrated on putting one foot out, the other. . . .

There was one dead tree in the clump. A bee tree, tall and thicker around at the base than a horse's girth. Too big to cut down with a bayonet, left-handed. Fargo leaned wearily on another tree, cocked his head upward. The whole thing was dead. Good firewood, couldn't find better. And it might as well be in Jackson, Moe, chopped up in stovewood lengths in front of Cletus Holloway's store, for all the good it was to him. His knees sagged suddenly and he pitched forward into the snow.

He wasn't out long. His face and his left hand were numb with cold. A spark of anger fanned inside and soon he was sitting up blowing snow from his beard and staring at the bee tree. He scooped a handful of snow and chewed it. It revived him some. There was a branch up there, fifteen feet or so off the ground. Thick, rotten, prime for burning. Well, he'd just get it.

A naturally right-handed man is in big trouble trying to do things from the other side. Throwing is hardest and that's what Fargo had to do——throw. A rock whirled at the end of the leather reins. He spun and threw so many times his shoulder ached before a lucky cast looped the thing around the limb he wanted. Then it was easy. Though he had to wait a little and recover some juice before taking a dally around a nearby tree, pulling down the big dead branch. He took it home.

Fire is a sort of magic in the wilderness. It holds back the cold and the animals; it protects and cooks for a man, and gives him something to dream of. It gives him life.

Fargo had got the butt of the big limb into the center of the shelter, started his fire under it. Now it smoldered strongly, throwing light and shadow on the walls. He had only to pull more of the limb into the cave to keep his fire going.

He sat in his issue shirt and stained breeches with the cavalry stripe, staring into the fire, fingering the Navy Colt. One shell left. It had taken one to start the fire. The blanket-coat belonging to the unknown teamster lay steaming on a rock. He was snug for the moment. The storm howled outside and sometime he would have to face the snow, the mountains again.

For now, he was secure. Soon he would sleep. The mess cup stood close to the fire, half-full of snow water and chunks of mule liver. It had begun to bubble and the rare smell of stewing meat filled the place. He would eat then sleep and go after the mule haunch the next day. He was going to need that meat.

His fingers idly traced the carved initials in the walnut stock of the Colt. C.W. Charlie Ward.

He would stay alive.

Silesia Bragg didn't live in Gault because Silesia

didn't do much of anything that other people did. Not that Gault was anything. But it was the only thing remotely like a town in more than a hundred miles of Dakota hills and canyons. A woman should live in town; everybody said so. Silesia didn't care much what other people said. Gault and its faceless mining people was no part of the reason she stayed on in the bleak high-canyon, grubbing a reluctant living out of the fall and stope Sam Bragg had hacked into the mountain.

Sam. Silesia straightened from the fire in the smoky cabin. Her eyes touched all the familiar things. Five years. Three of them without Sam. He'd gone into the war because he was Sam Bragg and all man. He wasn't ever coming back. It was still hard to think of all that slim, compact energy crushed on some rumbling field far from the hardrock high country he had loved. There wasn't much of him left. A miner's hat over the fireplace, the old rifle he'd left for her. She'd been wearing his clothes since she started to work the tiny mine herself and they no longer had anything to do with the man she had married. And they were a little tight, to tell the truth. Silesia smiled inside. Big Silesia and little Sam. A thump and a hard scraping noise against one wall pulled her out of the unaccustomed reverie.

"All right, Billy Buck. Don't get to pawin'."

She shrugged into a jacket, picked up the hand axe and stepped out into the sparkling morning. Harsh and white. It hadn't snowed since the big storm two weeks before but the white carpet was still thick over the entire canyon.

Silesia stood for a moment and looked out over her country. Not much. Her cabin was high and hung to the blind side of the canyon. Down-canyon and on the opposite side of the creek, she could make out the spatter of buildings that was Gault. And farther up, the mine entrance and the smelter. Smoke rose from the huts and cabins but not from the small refinery. Gault Mining and Smelting was on winter rations. The noisy creek, not frozen even in the coldest weather because it rushed too fast, cut a gash down the canyon floor. Gault clustered on the far side. On the blind side where Silesia was, there were a few placer diggings, snowbound now, and a bunch of other hard-scrabble outfits. None of them getting rich.

Silesia blew on her hands. They were strong hands, long-fingered and tough from swinging the short stope pick in the mine. Her eyes sought the large roof that marked MacCutcheon's store. Andy Mac said what she needed was a man. Not that he was volunteering—not with that hard-eyed wife of his. And Bugle. Wonder what it would be like to have a boy like that? She drew a lungful of the sharp air and felt her breasts thrust full and firm against Sam's shirt. Maybe she did need a man.

Billy Buck whinnied and Roger joined him. She started along the packed path to the stable lean-to. Be good to get into the ground again. Good for the ponies, too. All they did was eat and kick hell out of the stable. She stopped at the dwindling pile of fodder, snow-covered except for the side she'd been taking hay from. The axe cracked the layer of frost and she forked a double load into the low-roofed stable. Then she went inside, the acrid, warm smell of the ponies familiar and good.

"You're gettin' fat—both of you."

The two mine ponies swung shaggy heads to her, nickered softly. They were Shetlands and their winter hair was long and tangled. Delicate hooves and tiny bones, yet they could pull the heavy car up the inclined fall day after day loaded with ore and never seem to tire. Silesia pushed new hay where the animals could nuzzle. She tugged with rough affection at Billy Buck's stringy forelock.

"That hay's got enough frost in it so don't be stompin' around for water. Take you down later on."

She stepped back outside, bent to pick up the axe. When she straightened she saw the man.

He was big with wide, bowed shoulders and the hard flanks of a horseman. He had a bunch of harness wrapped around a filthy blanket coat and he was sliding stiff-legged down the side of the canyon wall near the mine entrance, both hands hanging loosely. Nobody she knew. Her hand tightened on the axe handle. The man was bearded with a streak of white through the center of his tangled black hair; he didn't seem to see her. His legs worked slowly and he staggered, moving toward the cabin. She stepped out in front of him and he stopped abruptly, rocking. She saw his eyes, then, dark and deep and sheltered by heavy bone. He stared, swaying.

"You want something, Mister?"

Silesia had to look up at him. It was an odd feeling for her. She gripped the axe.

"You hear? This is private property." His face was all bone and eyes and a matted beard. "Town's that way."

He said nothing for a long moment. Then something glinted far back in the shadowed eyes and he jerked a short nod, turned. He started down the rough slope, walking like a man on strings. He walked himself right into the ground, knees, hips, face. Silesia ran to him, sliding in the heavy snow. He was sprawled full length.

His feet were still making walking motions. . . .

Chapter 3

THE FIRST TIME Fargo woke he saw the woman. She was tall and young, with two heavy black braids pulled back over the tips of her ears and tied in back. She wore a man's clothes which were too tight for her ripe figure. He didn't try to speak; he was too grateful for the warmth and the protected feeling he had. Even though everything was kind of hard to focus on, the woman turned, maybe feeling his gaze. He allowed his eyes to close.

When he peered again through slitted lids she was busy at the fireplace, features highlighted by the hot blaze, stirring something in a pot. A good looking woman. He wanted to examine his body, assess damage, but some wary instinct kept him still. Nothing moved but his eyes.

Miner's cabin. There was a lamp cap over the fire, tools here and there and a scale and pestle for rough assays on a table. One big room but everything was solid and weathertight. One window covered with greased paper filtered hazy light into the semi-gloom. That and the fire was all the illumination the cabin had. The bed he lay on was wide and soft. Against the wall above it a small shelf held a Bible, the Navy Colt and a ball of linsey-woolsey skewered by a pair of knitting needles.

"You're awake."

The girl stood over him. Her face was shadowed, bending over as she was. Her hair made a halo with the light from behind.

"I—I didn't make it to town."

"You didn't," she said. "Don't move. That thing in your back is healed pretty good but you ain't ready to move sudden."

His hands searched under the feather comforter and he felt his stringy nakedness. His shoulder was stiff. He gathered himself.

"I've been a bother. . . ."

He lifted himself onto his elbows, swung his legs over the side of the bed. She stepped back, watching. He knew he was naked but it didn't matter, somehow. The woman's wise eyes watched him. He sat there, swaying. She smiled and it softened the capable lines of her face. Then she reached out a hand and pushed him lightly.

He seemed to fall back a long ways.

When he awoke again he did so all at once. It was day and the door was open pouring cold air and white glare into the cabin. There was a man bending over him and Fargo's eyes turned to the shelf above the bed; the Colt was there. The man looked down at him.

"Had enough sleep?"

Fargo got an impression of ruddy cheeks and a sweeping mustache.

"I'm Andy McCutcheon—run the store in town. Near as we got to a doctor, I guess. How you feel?"

Fargo cleared his throat, stirred in the soft bed.

"Where's the lady?"

"Silesia? She's outside. Turn over there and let's see that back."

The man's rough hands turned him. McCutcheon's fingers probed, moved his right arm around, testing it. There was no pain.

"Not sound but healed." The man helped him turn over again. He had a paunch and narrow shoulders but he was strong. "The ball's still in there. Ain't enough of a sawbones to be probing for lead but you'll do. What's your name?"

"Fargo."

The man grunted. "Well, Mister Fargo, reckon you know Miz Bragg saved your whistle. Picked you out of the snow, brought you here and been taking care of you for the last week. Good woman."

He seemed to expect an answer but Fargo had nothing to say. The storekeeper ran his eyes over him.

"You're big enough. What do you do?"

A shadow blocked the doorway momentarily and then the door closed. Silesia Bragg carried a bucket of water to the sink rack.

"Mule driver," Fargo said. "How about my back—can I travel?"

"Can if you want to. You got a piece of lead in there but the wound is healed. Better get yourself around three, four Silesia's meals—you're plumb ga'nt."

"Thank you for what you did."

McCutcheon shrugged. He pushed his hard belly out over Fargo reaching for the shelf behind the bed. His hand came back with the Colt. He hefted it, rubbed it.

"This yours?"

Fargo nodded.

"Know how to use it?"

Fargo reached up and took the pistol out of his hand, put it back on the shelf.

He said, "I'm owin' to you for doctoring on me. I'll pay you when I can."

The storekeeper tugged at his mustache, studied Fargo. He pulled up a rough chair and straddled it.

"I'll tell you something. You look like a man used to trouble. Now, no offense—but that's the way you come across. If it's so, you couldn't have come to a better place. Or picked a better time, for all of that."

The woman paused in her cooking preparations, stared at McCutcheon. Fargo heaved upward propping his shoulders against the rough wall. The effort cost him.

"I drive mules."

"You said. Now you take Gault. Small town—one big mine and no state or county government. This is a territory. Nobody cares where a man's come from, what's happened behind him. You think on that." He got up, shoved the chair back with a foot. "When you're feeling up to it, come see me in town."

Silesia stood next to the storekeeper suddenly, a wooden ladle in one hand. Her eyes were on a level with McCutcheon's.

"You finished, Andy Mac?"

He held up his hands, grinned. "All right. Don't shoot, I'm leaving."

Fargo said, "Thank you again."

McCutcheon waved it aside. "Man's hurt, you help him. You come see me like I said when you're up and around."

"Get on out of here with your backwoods politickin', Andy Mac." Silesia smiled at the man, walked to the door with him. "Tell Bugle to come up and help curry Billy Buck and Roger. Haven't seen him lately."

"Haven't heard that infernal horn of his, either, have you?" McCutcheon pulled open the door. "Bugle's had a little grippe. Be all right. I'll tell him what you said. And you remember what I said, Mister Fargo. . . ."

The door closed. The woman came back to the bed, her femaleness pushing at the flannel shirt, the canvas trousers. The room seemed smaller all at once. Silesia's eyes, round and unblinking, held his. Her lips were full and dark.

"Fargo." She said it slowly, tasting it.

"You pull me out of that snowdrift by yourself?"

Something changed in her face. "Yes. And I swing a pick and load ore and chop wood. You want to shave?"

"I'd like that." She was sensitive about her heftiness. He'd remember that.

"I'll fetch Sam's razor—put a pan in your lap and you can shave yourself."

"Thank you." He sat up in bed, holding himself rigid until the weakness passed. "Have I got some clothes someplace around?"

She came back with the shaving gear, a huck towel and a shallow basin.

"You got clothes. I cleaned them up some. But if you're going to be giving out you're a mule driver, better take them cavalry stripes off your breeches."

Thin and meandering veins of a metal too soft for tools and too dull for ornament were the reason for the existence of Gault, Dakota Territory. A mountain man by that name had stumbled onto gold in this obscure canyon some ten years before. A mild rush built a shack town. Then came the inevitable cartel with a little more money and a little more imagination and the smelter was built. Soon Gault was a one-company town, since exploration proved there was not very much gold and it was expensive to mine. The town started to dry up, almost disappeared. But the war came and suddenly the government had an interest and they sent a company of Federal troopers to see that the gold got mined to feed their war effort. They established order and maintained a climate where an independent miner could scratch a living out of the rock —if he had guts enough and a lot of faith.

The war years were good to Gault. Miles from anywhere, there had been no law at all until the military took over. Businesses came behind them, and families, all making the long and arduous wagon trip from Freemantle. A school was built. They planned a church but somehow it hadn't got done yet. The town grew, slowly but solidly.

Then the war ended and the company of troopers went away to their forts and posts and homes and Gault was alone again, a soft jugular in the wilderness.

Fargo walked along the odd, one-sided main street looking for McCutcheon's. The snow was melting and the street was a rutted mess of mud and slush. The boardwalk fronted the various establishments, dropping down with the canyon's slope by means of wooden steps here and there. The other side of the street was a black torrent of icy water. The air was cold with the approach of night.

Not much traffic. Couple of horses tied to the rack of the Hotel boardinghouse; mule hitch and an ore wagon before the lighted front window of an assay office. There were no saloons and only one eating house, one barber shop that Fargo could see. He fingered his own smooth chin. Good to be clean again. Silesia Bragg had done a job on his clothes and his right arm swung with just a trace of stiffness. Two weeks of her solid meals had helped. Pretty good shape, all in all. Weak, maybe, but that wouldn't last long.

McCutcheon's store was the biggest and most substantial of the town buildings. It sat off by itself beyond where the long boardwalk ended, on its own level space and fronted with a solid walk of split logs. There were high windows on the up-canyon side, a big one in front that was shuttered.

The mountain dark came sudden and absolute, like a blanket thrown over a lantern. Fargo paused on the log walk at McCutcheon's store and looked back at the gently-climbing town street. Lights and raw lumber, sod and stone. The creek murmured and shut out incidental sounds. Behind the main street, houses and shacks dotted the mountainside. All kinds of dwellings —from solid frame houses with glass to soddies with smoke holes in the roof. Below the store, the canyon lurched to the left with the creek and Fargo could not see past the bend. Nice town.

For a moment the tightly constructed defenses came down and Fargo got a bleak look at the things he had missed—hints of warmth and a familiar laugh, kid's shrilling in that special sound of youth, a place of his own that he knew was his. What had he to offer a town, any town? Red memories of war, daily weariness and hunger, the serious urgency to live through just one more day. He'd learned to do that. And very little more.

He shrugged off the feeling and pushed through the heavy door.

It was one big room and there were a number of men in it, but no noise. A hanging candle-wheel lit a single poker table in the far corner. Wall brackets held big lamps at either side of a counter-bar. Fargo got a coffee-pickles-machine oil smell blended with man and smoke and grease. There were shelves loaded with merchandise and stacks of harness, picks, shovels, gold cradles and paddy boards. All the clutter of a mining town store.

McCutcheon was behind the bar and most of the other men looked like miners or drovers. Except the one in front of the bar standing alone. He was a slim article with a chopped-looking face shadowed by a floppy hat. He held a drink half-way and his eyes followed Fargo without blinking.

"Mister McCutcheon. I came by like you said."

McCutcheon's frown was puzzled, then quickly gone. "Fargo. Didn't recognize you without all that beaver." His ruddy cheeks pushed up in a grin then sagged suddenly with a quick glance at the black-hatted man. "You come for that drink I promised, eh? Right up, right up."

Fargo felt the familiar tightening inside. Something was wrong. Shouldn't have anything to do with him but a man never knew. He watched the paunchy McCutcheon rattle a bottle against a glass, fill it slopping over. He turned a casual glance on the room. There was no movement. None. The poker game was silent and still. Casual standers were stiff and studiously not looking at the bar. The slim man put his glass down with a thump, wheeled smoothly towards Fargo and pushed his coat back from a low-tied, black gun. His eyes were dark chips in the rough-angled face.

"So you're McCutcheon's new man."

Fargo took a slow breath, said carefully, "I'm not anybody's man."

"McCall, listen," the storekeeper said. "You're wrong. This man has no—"

"Shut up, Mac." McCall's voice was Texas, but not soft. "You been talkin' it around you got a hotrock to take Judson's place. About citizen's posses and burnin' down the lower camp. Well, I figure this is your Honcho."

Fargo said, "I don't know a soul in this room except him, Mister. And I only saw him once. I don't know who you are and I don't know what you're talking about."

"Don't you? Open your coat. Open it!"

McCutcheon looked sick; his face was gray and mottled. Fargo unhooked the buttons of the mackinaw with his good hand. Nobody else moved. The coat fell open and the butt of the Colt was right there sticking up from his waistband.

McCall smiled. "Well, now. You want that drink, Honcho? Better drink it now 'cause I'm gonna kill you right quick."

Fargo's eyes went from man to man around the room; nobody was going to do anything, that was evident. He faced McCall, kept his hands away from the front of his coat.

"This is stupid. Nobody goes around shooting people for no reason."

"You want a reason, Honcho—make you feel better? Put it down I don't like them pants you're wearin'." He jerked his head toward the door. "Let's go outside, you and me. You'll be able to tell 'em up there in heaven—or wherever you go—that you shot it out with Sudden Jack McCall."

"Wait!" It was a small man with prominent teeth and wearing a suit and tie, a hard hat. "McCall, you can't get away with this. Pushing people, leaning on them. You can't do it!"

McCall stood by the door, righthand thumb hung in his belt. He was a little drunk Fargo realized, and enjoying every minute of this.

"You want to take ol' Honcho's place, Mister Mayor? Humh? Say you don't, huh. . . ." He exploded with sudden laughter, suddenly stopped. "You pukes make me sick! Talk, that's all you do and you don't do that good."

"Jack, listen," the little man said. "I never saw this man before. Whatever you heard, I'm the Mayor and if we hired a new Marshal I'd know it, wouldn't I? Leave him alone."

Sudden Jack McCall stared at Fargo, not giving attention to anyone else. "Maybe so. Whoever he is, he's bad news. Outside, Honcho. I ain't tellin' you again."

He pulled open the door, stood waiting. Fargo's face was bitter. His gaze swept the room.

"What the hell kind of town is this? A dozen grown

men and you let an imitation bad man make dirt out of you!"

He moved to the door in a thick silence. McCall held the heavy door open, eyes wary. Fargo looked back at the sweating storekeeper.

"Thanks again, McCutcheon."

And he drove his elbow into McCall's flat belly as hard as he could, jumped for the door and hit running. Two steps on the boardwalk and he launched his body into a flat dive out into the mud-rutted street. A gun went off behind him. He landed, twisting and rolled desperately in the gook. A bullet fanned his hair and he saw the blast and Jack McCall standing black against McCutcheon's storefront with his pistol belching fire.

Then he had the Navy Colt in his left hand and was lifting it, trying to center it for one good shot, and it had to be good because one shell was all there was in the Colt. In a confused flash he saw McCutcheon in the doorway behind the gunman with a shotgun, heard him shout and McCall begin to turn.

Fargo fired. McCall had wheeled to snap a shot at the storekeeper and Fargo's ball took him in the middle of the spine.

Sudden Jack was dead before he hit. He never knew that he lived up to his name far better in death than he ever had in life. . . .

Chapter 4

"You're a big help, McCutcheon."

The man raised stricken eyes from the figure of Jack McCall, the dollar-sized hole in his back.

"I was—I was trying to—" His eyes slid to the door which was still closed; none of the others had ventured out since the shooting. "You shot him in the back, Fargo."

"Don't be dumb. He spun around to shoot you. And you're not making me forget you got me into this, McCutcheon. You started it and now you don't like the way it turned out."

"But in the back! There's a difference. . . ."

"He's dead and I'm not. That's the only difference that counts."

The door opened slowly and the little man with the chipmunk face stuck his head out.

"What happened?"

McCutcheon roused, stepped to the door. "Prudhomme—have somebody get a blanket from the top shelf behind the counter. Hurry up."

"But what happened?"

The storekeeper blocked the man's view of the body, said, "Fargo killed Jack McCall. Get that blanket." He closed the door. Moving quickly, he threw the unfired shotgun to Fargo, bent to the body and wrestled it over so the bullet hole was hidden. Sudden Jack's eyes had dried and the moonlight glazed them.

"What're you doing?"

"Just do as I say," McCutcheon muttered, as a man came out with a blanket. He was a youngish miner, sturdy and competent-looking, with steady eyes. "Bring it here, Lloyd. Let's get him wrapped up. For God's sake, Fargo, go have a drink! It's done!"

Fargo watched in silence as they swathed the boneless man-body in the new trade blanket. Then he went inside.

Everyone clamored and asked questions. Fargo got a drink and kept shaking his head. They all wanted to congratulate him at once. He'd gunned down the worst of the Spoilers—a man whose reputation stretched from Texas to San Francisco. Now they'd be able to handle the Lower Camp—now Gault needn't be overrun by riff-raff, the dregs of both armies.

More people kept crowding into the store, drawn by

the excitement. McCutcheon returned from his body-hiding chore and pounded on the bar for attention.

"Listen! Listen, everybody." It got quiet. The little storekeeper's mustache quivered. "Y'all know what happened. Sudden Jack McCall is dead. And here's the man that killed him."

He pointed to Fargo. A murmur began but McCutcheon pounded it down.

"Wait! Of all the rowdies down below, McCall and Hobie Spencer were the only ones to worry about. Well, Fargo's taken care of Sudden Jack. I say we ought to give him the job to finish!"

"Sure! Give him Judson's job," a miner offered.

"Now wait just a minute." It was Foster Prudhomme, the chipmunk-looking mayor. "A man comes stumbling out of the hills, we know nothing about him. Who he is—where he comes from. And you want to give him a badge. Make him responsible for the lives of our wives and children. I'm against it. I will so vote!"

McCutcheon shouted through the rising murmur. "Is it the man you're against, Prudhomme? Or the fact that I propose him for the job?"

Then everyone was talking at once. Fargo sipped his drink and watched. Ten minutes before some of them had been scared and silent, willing to let a stranger face death in a game he hadn't even entered. Now they were jockeying for position and taking high moral tones about it. He turned away. Lloyd, the miner who'd brought the blanket, caught his eye and grinned. He held up a bottle, nodded toward the deserted poker table.

"They do come on, don't they now," he said, and the 'come' sounded like 'coom.' They sat, the bottle between them on the table. "Lloyd Dempster. You'll be Fargo—as everyone in town knows by now."

Fargo took the man's hand. "Irish?"

"Welsh. Good Wales mining stock. Though I'd thought the bit of an accent was gone by now."

Fargo smiled, "It isn't. Tell me about this Spoiler Camp. What is it?"

"Ah. You'd have to know a bit about the mining. You see there's tailings and rock we call bad-crush—not worth even hauling to the smelter. Well, it goes in the creek, like as not, and the current carries it off. Spoils, it's called, d' you see." Dempster hauled out a stubby briar, began packing it with work-roughened fingers. "Now—there's them that run cradles and riffle-boards down around the bend apiece, taking what gold they can from the spoils."

"That McCall, he didn't strike me as a miner."

Lloyd shook his head, busied himself getting the briar lit and billowing smoke. "Never hit a lick in his life, that one. That's how the camp grew up down there, from the spoils. Not much, as you'll see. Soddies and tarpapers—one decent building, Savannah's place. What it's become is another tale. . . ."

He talked on and Fargo listened, letting the ebb and flow of the big argument wash around them. The lower camp had become early on the place where undesirables congregated. A whorehouse sprang up, and a saloon. Soon it became necessary to hire a town marshal and hold miner's court to keep the trouble down. Then, a month before, Jack McCall had killed the Marshal—a man named Judson—and the threat of the Spoilers touched everyone in Gault. Suddenly they could feel the simmering ugliness so close to them. And lately drifters and deserters from both armies had begun swelling the lower camp, now that the war was finished. Something had to be done. Everyone agreed to that but could not come close to agreement on what or how.

"Until now, d'you see. Whether to hire you or not. The mine manager, Prudhomme, on the one side, McCutcheon on the other."

"And in the middle?"

Dempster's face made a sour expression around his pipe. "Aye—the people as always. But tell me—" He leaned forward, fixed Fargo with his steady gaze. "I've heard no one ask you yet. D'you want the job, man?"

"I'm no gunman, Lloyd."

"That's the hell of it, then. None of us are. I'm a mining man. A good one, and my father before me. But sometimes when those sods spread their filth, rub decent people with their greed—then a man wishes he had the way of weapons, the strength. Like tonight. . . ." He looked away. "I'm not proud of that, Mister Fargo. But—there's Nellie and the babies, and——" He shook his head, downed his drink.

"Fargo." McCutcheon came toward him, face flushed and shining. "We've voted and it's legal and proper. We're offering you the job of keeping the peace in Gault!"

They waited. Fargo looked at Lloyd Dempster for a long moment. Then he turned back to the expectant crowd.

"Why not?" he said.

It was as good a place as any to wait for Charlie.

Freemantle was the largest town in the Dakota hills and Charlie Ward headed straight for it after his discharge. He'd had more than enough service time and with the army de-mobbing getting out had been the easiest part. Wasn't much of a town at that. Streets full of muddied snow, and shrill kids throwing snowballs. It wasn't St. Louis. But it had a U.S. land office and that's where Charlie went after he'd stabled his horses.

The man at the government land office in Freemantle fussed with the stack of maps. He peered over half-spectacles.

"What'd you say your name was?"

"Ward. You heard me the first time. Now do I get to see those maps or do I take my army discharge to your district commissioner and tell him how much help you've been to one of our country's heroes?"

The fussy man polished his spectacles calmly. "You needn't lean on me, Mr. Ward. That's what I'm here for—to give information and service. However, when a man tells me he is a recently discharged veteran interested in establishing a hauling business . . . in these mountains . . . in mid-winter. . . ."

Charlie pushed down a quick surge of irritation. "Can I see the maps?"

"Of course." The little man replaced his spectacles, blinked over them. "What is your purpose—really?"

"It's none of your business, old man." Charlie's rusty voice filled the small office.

The little man smiled. "Ah, but I *am* an old man. And this is a dull job. You see, Mister Ward—or should I say Sergeant Ward? When a man reaches a certain age he must take his romance, his excitement where he can." The lively eyes twinkled behind the specs. "You see? To me you represent—oh, adventure, mystery—all of the things forever denied me by an unkind fate."

Charlie Ward stared at the man for a long moment. When he spoke there was no mistaking the menace. "Old man, if you don't give me what I want—and right now!—you're likely to get more excitement than you can handle."

The light died in the little man's eyes. He bent to the stack of curled survey maps and began sorting them mechanically.

Half an hour later, Charlie Ward walked slowly around his two horses in the chewed-up yard of the town's livery barn. Pack animal was carrying pretty heavy. But then he had a long way to go, maybe. And rough country to go over. The yard, like Freemantle's streets, was a riot of mud and dirty snow. His cavalry boots sucked in the mess and he knew a soldier's vague irritation. Mud and snow. Seemed like his last five years had been spent mostly in mud.

The wind was chilly. Charlie's muttonchops stirred with it. His noncom's eye went over his equipment automatically. In his mind he recited the seven names he'd gotten at the land office, wondered which to start with. He had found the spot on the maps where he'd last seen Fargo. Then, drawing a two-hundred mile circle to the north and west, with the original spot at the edge of the circle, he'd noted the names of all the towns, settlements, trading posts within it. Just seven. In this country that could mean months of traveling to reach them all. Nothing but mountains and canyons, more mountains and canyons.

Sanctuary. Odd name for a town—and maybe Fargo would pick it for that reason. Frenchman's Creek—tin mining. Tender Butte—Indian post. Two Bows—another. Welcome—trading post on the upper Platte. Deadwood—a good sized town, and Charlie decided in that instant he would try Deadwood first. Last was Pinckneyville—a gold camp.

"Ready to go, Mister?" The lank-haired hostler, too lightly dressed for the weather, stood before him shivering.

"You grain 'em?"

"Yessir—like you said. Put a half-sack in the pack. I rubbed 'em down good, Mister."

Ward yanked on a cinch strap, rocked the McClellan saddle back and forth on his mount's back. Might as well get started. He reached into his pocket.

"That's three dollars, Mister." The cold kid jittered in the freezing mud. "I rubbed 'em, fed 'em grain. . . ."

Ward gave him two silver dollars.

There seemed to be a lot of commotion at the Drover's corral next door. A wagon had driven up a while ago and there'd been men running here and there ever since. One man had been carried into the Drayage Company office. Now he noticed a portly man with a doctor's bag hurrying into the same door.

"What's goin' on over there?"

The kid was sullen; he dragged a raw wrist over a drop of moisture at the end of his nose. "I dunno. . . ."

Ward sighed and gave the kid another dollar.

"Ain't nothin', much," the kid said. "One of their rigs like to got snow buried tryin' to get to a mining camp. Drover got some chilblains, is all. They was dumb. Everybody knows can't nobody get through up to Gault til' the weather breaks. But them, they wanted to get rich with a load before everybody. Wonder they didn't all—"

Charlie shook the kid into silence. "What was that name? The mining camp?"

"G-Gault. Hey Mister, I ain't done nothin'. Let me go!"

Ward released him, took a five-dollar gold piece from his pocket and held it where the kid could see it.

"Answer a couple questions? All right?"

The kid nodded eagerly, snuffling.

"How far is this Gault?"

" 'Bout oh, maybe hundred, hundred-ten miles. But it's rough, Mister. Jist cain't get there when the snow's down."

Ward's mind went over the list the old man in the land office had prepared for him. Sanctuary, Frenchman's Creek, Tender Butte, Welcome, Two Bows, Deadwood, Pinckney. No Gault anywhere in that.

"What direction's it in?"

"Thataway." The kid pointed; his eyes stuck to the small gold piece. "North and west—up the Platte to where Gault Creek meets it. Ain't no trouble to *find*— jist cain't get there this time of year. Kin I have the money?"

"In a minute. Is there anything special about this camp? Anything—you know, that people talk about?"

"Special? It ain't but a comp'ny town way the hell out, is all." The kid danced, blowing on his hands, gaze never leaving the half-eagle. "You mean like everybody sayin' that's where the bad 'uns—deserters 'n all—that's where they're holin' up 'cause it's so hard to get to? Is that what you mean, Mister?"

That son-of-a-bitch in the land office! Anger rose

but Ward forgot it as soon as he recognized the other feeling welling up in him—certainty. He gave the gold piece to the kid.

"Get some boots. Good soldier keeps his feet dry."

But the kid was halfway to somewhere by then, ruined shoes hardly touching the sucking mud.

Charlie Ward rode out of Freemantle at dusk, after having spent a profitable half-hour in the Drayage Company office. Cost him a bottle of whiskey but he knew how to get to the gold camp called Gault. They'd warned him, long and loud, that the canyon was a "piss-whistler" in winter. No chance for a wagon at all. A man with a good horse and a pack animal, now, might have a chance.

If he cared enough. . . .

Chapter 5

THE JAIL WAS one of the few stone structures in town. On a back street, it was up-canyon and slightly up the slope from McCutcheon's store. From the small wooden porch Fargo could see over the roofs of the main street buildings, both up-canyon and down for quite a ways. It was early morning and the first shift was assembling up at the main shaft. There was no activity on the street below.

Fargo stood on the porch in shirtsleeves and stockinged feet wondering what had brought him out. Then he heard it again, muted and wind-carried but unmistakably the lifting notes of the charge being blown on a cavalry bugle. He frowned. Seemed to be coming from the rimrock behind the town. Shivering slightly in the morning chill, he walked to the edge of the porch.

At that moment there was a shrill whistle from the town. Fargo saw McCutcheon standing behind his store waving at the rimrock. He followed the direction of the man's gestures and saw a small figure up there, clambering downward. The sun glinted on a brass object hanging from the boy's neck and Fargo realized that he'd been hearing the storekeeper's boy practicing his bugle. He smiled and went back inside. Kid was pretty good.

It was cold inside, too. Fargo set about building a fire in the ancient castiron stove which centered the big single room. The backwall was solid bars fronting the two small cells; one sidewall held posters and a hanging blanket of Indian design and the other a sleeping alcove with dusty muslin draping the opening. A rolltop desk sat flush against the frontwall in one corner. On the wall at the entrance was a gun rack. It held a pair of shotguns, a new-looking Henry and an old Sharps. All were dusty and neglected, as was everything in the place. The cot he'd slept on was crude and the blankets had reminded him of long campaigns when everything gets musky and rank.

The fire started to burn well. He forced a chunk of spruce in on top of the roaring kindling and shut the door. He'd had worse billets. Lots of them. His gaze fell on the empty holster hanging on the alcove wall. He got the Navy Colt and tried it in the stiff scabbard. Colt was too small. Marshal Judson had packed a forty-four. He hung the thing back on the wall, leaving the Colt in it.

Someone rattled the door. There was a front window but he'd seen nothing cross it. The bumping came again and with it a treble, "Hey, Marshal. You in there?"

Fargo stepped into his boots and opened the door. A solemn-faced ten-year-old carrying a basket and a tin pail stood there.

"Got some bait for you," he said, looking up. "Ma sent it. I'm Andrew McCutcheon Junior but you kin call me Bugle."

Fargo nodded. "Heard you this morning. Come on in."

The boy carried his burdens to the deal table, put them down. His face was red-cheeked and shining. He brought a fresh smell into the musty room.

"Ain't but some biscuits and strap. Coffee's hot, though. You hungry?"

He was, he realized. Still hadn't recovered from the weeks in the mountains. He was a big man and had always eaten more than his share. The biscuits were hot and good, filled with melting butter. He swabbed them in the thick molasses, chewed gratefully. The boy watched with wide, bright eyes. Fargo poured a cup of the steaming coffee.

"You eat?"

"Yes, sir. We ate real early." He swiveled, boy-like, eyes darting. "There's your ol' Colt, huh? Pa said you got Sudden Jack 'fore he blinked. And he was fast. Faster'n Hobie Spencer, everybody says."

Fargo pushed the basket back and settled at the table, cradling his coffee. The boy jittered, hanging on to the other side of the table.

"You must be slicker'n wet clay, Marshal. Everybody says so. 'Cept ol' Prudhomme and he's just worried about the mine and nothin' else. Everybody knows that."

"How about your Pa, Bugle? What's he worried about?"

"Ain't nothin' worries Pa. Less it'd be me blowin' my horn in town. He whacked me good last time." He paused, considering; then, "Well, he wants to be Mayor, I reckon. Prudhomme beat him last time."

"Everybody know that, too, huh?"

"Sure." Bugle sped to the gun rack, looked up at the pieces. "Better get you some oil on these here. Judson, he didn't take no kind of care of things."

"Bugle...." The boy came back to the table, opening his coat in the warmth. "You think these Spoilers are bad people? I mean, there's your Pa, other men . . . they could stop them if they had to, couldn't they?"

Bugle squirmed and his face became grave. It wasn't a fair question for a ten-year-old. "Them Spoilers is gunmen. They just *take* what they want."

"Think I should go after 'em,—clean 'em out?"

"Oh, you won't have to do that. They'll be comin' for you. Maybe right quick."

"That's something else everybody knows, isn't it?"

"Sure. Crimey, you killed Sudden Jack. They ain't agoin' to let you get away with that. Kin I take the pail and basket? Ma told me to bring 'em back."

"You take 'em. And tell your Ma thank you kindly." He stood suddenly and stretched; the room was getting hot.

The boy said, "You ought to get you a hat, cover up that white in your hair. How come that?"

Fargo got his mackinaw from the alcove, turned the damper on the stove. "Tell you sometime. Come on— walk you down to the street."

Fargo opened the door, waited while the boy edged outside, loaded down with the basket and tin pail. He looked up at Fargo, eyes round and questioning.

"What's wrong?"

"Well—Pa said this morning . . . maybe you wouldn't stay. You will, won't you, Mister Fargo?"

Fargo thought of the many places he'd been, how much he'd left behind. He buttoned his coat.

"Yes, Bugle, I'm going to stay. Now that's something everybody *doesn't* know, isn't it?"

The boy grinned, nodded. Fargo pulled the door shut and the two stood for a moment on the porch, the small boy and the big man. Bugle reached up and touched the simple, five-pointed star on Fargo's coat.

"You gonna wear that? Makes an awful good target."

Andy McCutcheon knew when he opened the store that morning that Foster Prudhomme would be around sometime during the day to continue the argument about Fargo. He looked forward to it and made small bets in his mind about when he'd arrive. Foster, now, he just couldn't stand the thought someone else might have more influence on the town than he had. It was understandable. As the resident manager for the Gault Mining and Smelting Company he had a lot of authority. And he was a good man. Ran the operation profitably and still gave the miners two or three shifts a week even in the dead of winter so they could feed their families. But he had no real stake in Gault; for him it was just a job. He couldn't know how it was for a man who'd helped subdue this mountain, fought hunger and greed and his own doubts to make a settlement grow where none had a right to be.

"I know." He wasn't aware that he'd spoken aloud. His fingers sorted and folded merchandise while his eyes looked inward at the memory of that first killing winter on the mountain. He'd been one of the pitiful handful of survivors and he had made up his mind right then to quit digging for gold like the rest and build something solid. Something a man could depend on against the elements—against the world, too. So he'd built the store, worked hard to make it pay. It was his town. Not Foster Prudhomme's, not anybody's.

"Mine!" He slammed a hand on the counter.

"What is yours, Mr. McCutcheon?"

His wife stood in the doorway to their living quarters. She was a thin woman, still young, with sallow skin and bunned yellow hair showing gray. Andy stared. In the grip of the past, he saw the laughing girl she once was, delicate and fine. He felt a twinge of remorse. Now the laughing eyes were cold.

"Why, the store, Caroline. The place here. . . ."

"And the trouble—is that yours, too? Or may the rest of us share that?"

He sighed. "We've been over this 'til it's shredded, Caroline. We ain't leaving Gault! It's our home."

The pale lips thinned. "Your home; not mine. And

not my son's, if God delivers us through this evil winter. I need some salt and dried apples."

He turned away, silent.

Lloyd Dempster came through the front door, moving fast. His earnest young face was tight.

"Andy Mac—Prudhomme sent me to fetch you to the mine, man. Important, it is."

Andy nodded without hesitation, grateful for the interruption.

The mine office was in one end of the company bunkhouse near the main shaft entrance. The building was solid; stone halfway and split log from there. McCutcheon heard the chuff and whine of the steam mule hauling ore cars up the main fall and knew a shift was underground. Part of one, anyway. The smelter was quiet, as was the crusher, so it wouldn't be a full shift. He kicked mud and snow off his boots and went into the office behind Lloyd Dempster.

"Shut the door," Foster Prudhomme said. "And drop the bar."

The little man was behind his desk, a scatter of papers before him. He wore his customary shirt and vest, but no collar, no tie. The familiar hard hat lay on the floor with a dent in it and his thinning hair was rumpled.

"Foster," McCutcheon said, "you look like a one arm man with an off-side itch. So tell me how and why it ain't gonna do me no good havin' a marshal appointed over your objection."

"Turn it off, Andy. This isn't the time." The Mayor's voice was soft, a little tired. He watched Lloyd Dempster bar the door, then went on. "I need your help. Open the safe, Lloyd."

The dominant feature of the office was the huge metal lock cabinet bolted to the stone in the far corner. It was a good safe, with twin doors and locking both by key and combination. Prudhomme worried his lower lip with chipmunk teeth while the stocky Welsh miner pulled the already unlocked doors apart. Mc-

Cutcheon just stared. Inside, were crosshatched stacks of refined gold ingots. A hundred or more. Plus canvas and leather bags of all shapes and description which Andy knew belonged to independent miners, business men—even to himself. It was the wealth of Gault and the reason for its being.

"I've never seen it all like that," Andy said.

"Few people have. What you see is the whole of our refined product for the winter. All of it. It represents another year of operation for the company. Another year of employment for the miners. . . ."

". . . and another year of life for Gault."

Prudhomme nodded. He swung back to the desk, pushed aimlessly at the papers. "I've never told you this—mostly because we're always too busy shouting to talk. But the company wanted to close down this operation when the army pulled out. Oh, don't blame the company officials, Andy. It's just business. Hardrock mining for gold in a low-yield area like this one is expensive and chancey. Lose a big shipment and there goes the profit for an entire year—maybe two. You know that."

McCutcheon nodded. There was a scary, liquid feeling spreading inside him. When he spoke his voice seemed to roar in his ears.

"You're sayin' they'll close the goddam mine if we lose this. You're sayin' the town will die like a grounded trout and you're right! But why should we lose it? Why?" He knew he was speaking faster, louder, but he couldn't stop. "The Spoilers, Prudhomme? Is that what you're afraid of? They're bold, God knows, but not *that* bold!"

"They're not?" The little man snapped it. "What happened to Judson? How many times have they terrorized the town in drunken mobs and nobody lifted a finger? Ahhh—" He jerked his arm in a chopping motion. "Forget all that. My office manager, Winkle—you know him? Tell him about it, Lloyd."

The young miner seemed stiff, reluctant. After a

moment, he began to speak, twisting his hat in rough hands. "I went down there last night, d'you see? The lower camp, to Savannah's. Some of the boys do, you know and with my Nell being pregnant and all—" He stopped, head lowered.

"Get on with it, Lloyd, a man's a man."

"Aye. Well—I saw him down there. Winkle. I didn't go in that ratty saloon, but peek through a wall crack I did. There they were the dirty lot of 'em, wranglin' and millin' around fit to cork. Hobie Spencer, black in the face he was—and that heathen No-britches howlin' and bashin' at things with that mace he's got. And right in the middle of the mess was this Winkle, the office man. Drunker than the Governor's duck, d'you see, and one of Savannah's ladies on his knee." Lloyd put the abused hat on his head, got out a black briar. "That's the lot. Save me comin' to Mister Prudhomme this mornin' and Winkle not come back to work. And the key to the safe missin' and all. . . ."

Andy's chest felt empty and cold. "You mean— Winkle has a key? And he knows the combination? Then why didn't they steal it last night? Hobie Spencer's no fool. He knows you'll find out about the key today."

Prudhomme nodded. "I think they meant to do it last night. Sudden Jack McCall was to be the diversion. If it hadn't been Fargo, then someone, anyone. Just to make a fuss. When McCall got killed, it panicked them. But they won't stay panicked long." He gestured toward the safe. "Not with that to bring 'em. And Winkle telling how much there is."

"Then Fargo saved it." Andy felt a note of triumph through the confusion. "My Marshal. They don't know who he is; maybe they'll just go on bein' scared of him and leave us alone."

The little man looked at him steadily. "You're a fool. We've got to move the gold. Now. Today. The three of us. There's an old worn out stope on three level. It'll be safe there. Will you help or not?"

"Sure. Sure I'll help. But Fargo. Shouldn't we get him, too?"

"Fargo's a dead man, Andy. You know it as well as I do. They'll come for him first, then the gold. And they'll come tonight."

Silesia was tired. She followed the loaded ore car up the slight incline of the main fall, extinguishing lamps as she went. Billy Buck and Roger had needed the work; they had strained while climbing the slope. It was good to work. Good for the animals and good for her. It had been her anodyne when she learned that Sam Bragg had been killed. Work. Hard, constant, mind-dulling work.

Outside, the air was sharp and cold. A pale, watery sun hung over the western rim. Be dusk soon. Silesia dumped the ore car, unhitched the steaming ponies. Roger nickered and rubbed a shoulder against her. She slapped him affectionately.

"Howdy."

She turned quickly and saw him standing beside the mine entrance—just like the first time. Fargo. Her cheeks grew hot and she was conscious of the rough clothes, the thick boots. She swept off the miner's hat and shook loose her hair. He was beside her then, bulking tall, hair blown wild and the smell of outdoors on him. She leaned on Roger.

"Mrs. Bragg," he said. "Didn't mean to startle you. Been taking a look around today. The lower camp, the rimrock on both sides. Sort of a scouting trip. Since I don't know much about being a lawman, I figured I better act like a soldier and get a look at the terrain." He tapped the star pinned to his blanket coat. "You heard about this?"

"I heard. And about that McCall. Damn Andy McCutcheon to hell!"

She saw the tiny smile begin, slowly erasing the deep ridges on both sides of his nose. He had a nice smile. Her own lips moved in response.

"Not that bad, Silesia. Man's got to do something."

"But not buy somebody else's trouble. It's not your fight, Fargo."

He shrugged and his expression grew bleak. "Maybe not. It comes to me, though, I've been doing that for a long time—fighting battles I really had no stake in. One more won't hurt."

"They won't help you. The men down there. You know that, don't you? They expect you to fight for all of them. They won't lift a finger—not even to save themselves."

"They'd help if they knew how. They're just not fighters. Miners, business people, family men—violence is foreign to them, Silesia. Fighting and killing doesn't come easy. It's hard to take a human life. It's against nature and it needs a special sort of man. I'm that sort. They're not."

She looked up into his face for a long moment; there was truth there, and hurt. She wanted to soothe the hurt, make that deep self-mockery in the dark eyes disappear. She lifted a hand, touched the star lightly.

"Man has killin' to do," she said, "ought to eat good. You take care of the ponies and I'll fix something. All right?"

The firelight softened the harshness of the cabin making it homey and warm. Fargo sat by the table staring into the blaze while Silesia cleared the dishes, put the room to rights. She watched him as she worked, stealing glances. There was a strength about him you could feel. Like a force. He made her feel almost delicate.

During the meal she had asked about the streak of white in his hair. He told her about the three terrible weeks he'd spent in the mountains. No food except mule meat and a few roots and some moss. The daily search for shelter to keep alive just one more night. She hadn't asked how he came to be in the mountains, wounded and without an outfit. If he wanted her to know, he'd tell her.

"More coffee?"

He looked around slowly, shook his head. "No. Good meal, Silesia. And I'm an expert since I've had so many bad ones. Sit down. You look tired."

"Wait," she said. "I've got a hat, an old one of my —of Sam's. I want you to have it."

It was a flat-crowned Stetson and it wasn't old at all. It was a little small for Fargo but he could wear it. He thanked her solemnly. Then she walked around the table to her seat. He took her hand, held it gently, looking up at her.

"Silesia." He said her name like a caress, and she swayed. "I'm not up on courting. That's something else the war didn't leave much time for. But I want you to know—you're very pretty. You're about the prettiest girl I ever saw."

"Fargo, I— Oh, my God. . . ."

She was in his arms then and it didn't matter that she wore men's clothes and had rough hands. With melting lips she searched his face, his hard mouth, and her arms held him tight, tight. Her breathing was a roar and her full breasts grew taut against the shirt's restraint.

"Silesia." His voice was thick. "I've been hungry a long time."

Her whisper was fierce. "A woman's just no 'count without a man."

His lips crushed hers; there was heat and urgency and the thudding of blood in the silent night.

The door slammed inward. Bugle McCutcheon stood in the doorway framed against the blackness outside.

"Marshal! The Spoilers—they're here!"

Chapter 6

THREE OF THEM came to McCutcheon's store. Four others had ridden on past, continuing up canyon. The leader of the three was Roy Spencer, mean as a snake and looking like one with his hooded eyes and long, thin frame. His body appeared boneless but Andy knew there was a wild strength in the man. His brother was the worst of the Spoilers, one of the genuine bad men of the times, and Roy never stopped trying to live up to Hobie's example, surpass it if possible. The second one (McCutcheon knew him only as O'Neill) was short-legged and long-armed, wearing a filthy Confederate uniform of sorts. His face was all flaring beard and pock marks.

The third was No-britches. He was an Indian; no one knew what kind. Dull black hair braided over each shoulder and a hawk face dominated by black eyes in which red bits smoldered. Despite his name, he did wear breeches—but with the entire seat cut away. His only weapon was a knout—a fist-sized chunk of hard rock covered with braided leather and swung at the end of two feet of rawhide attached to his wrist. He was never without it. McCutcheon had seen him snap a four-by-four porch support with one blow of the thing.

They had entered with a rush, fanning out to cover all exits. The only customers had been Lloyd and Nellie Dempster.

"Well, storekeeper," Roy Spencer said. "Here we are. Been lookin' for us, storekeeper?"

McCutcheon shook himself, tried to force a smile. "You know you're always welcome here, Roy. Always welcome."

"Stop that bullshit! Get some liquor out here. No-britches!"

The Indian, prowling in the dark rear of the store, glided up.

"One drink for you," Spencer said. "Understand? One."

No-britches nodded, the red glow deepening in his mad eyes. Andy poured quickly, his mind whirling in panic. Bugle and Caroline were in the back. *Oh, God, don't let them come in here. Don't let them....*

The Indian downed his drink with one flip of his wrist, began prowling again, his knout dangling almost to the floor. Spencer drank two quick ones, moved to the door while O'Neill had his, then took one back to his post at the door. His dull eyes never left Nellie Dempster. Lloyd put an arm around his wife, edged as close to the wall as he could.

"All right, storekeeper—where is he? Where's your pet marshal, huh? The bad fella that killed Jack McCall?"

"I don't know. I haven't seen him since last night."

Spencer's hard hand exploded against his face and Andy stumbled back against the shelves. Real fear touched him. They were out of control for sure.

"Don't lie, storekeeper. I want to see him, that marshal. Here—right now!" His hooded eyes swung to the Dempsters. "O'Neill—get the woman."

O'Neill's eyes gleamed. He grabbed Nellie Dempster by the wrist, pulled viciously. Lloyd cried out and started after them. Spencer's pistol jumped out, centered the miner.

"Hold it, Mole!"

The hammer came back.

"Please." Lloyd's eyes were tear-filled; his tough workman's hands clawed in front of him. "Please, Mister Spencer. She's going to have a baby. Please...."

The grunting O'Neill had Nellie pushed against the door with his body. His hands fondled her and his breath whistled shrilly. Lloyd trembled. Spencer stood grinning, pistol cocked and pointed.

"Listen. . . ." McCutcheon was surprised to hear his own voice. "Spencer, look. Let the girl go home. She's no good to you. I'll get the marshal. I promise. I'll get him!"

Nellie Dempster started crying. No-britches lifted a bottle of whiskey off the counter behind Spencer's back and disappeared into the store's gloom.

"No," Roy Spencer said, watching O'Neill nuzzle the woman. "You stay here. You, Mole—you want to go get the marshal?"

Lloyd Dempster's face was anguished. His hands trembled. He shook his head. "I—I won't leave my wife."

Nellie broke away from the bearded outlaw, sobs racking her. O'Neill caught her, pushed her to the wall again.

Andy said, "Stop him, Roy, for the love of God! Let her go. Listen, let her go home. And I'll—I'll send my son for Fargo. He's young. He can run. He'll bring him right away."

Spencer shot a look at Andy, then nodded. "No-britches! Come here." The Indian was there in a flash, swishing his knout and making guttural noises in his throat. "O'Neill——get away from her!" The bearded man didn't hear; his face was buried in the hysterical girl's bosom. Spencer nodded to the Indian. "Get him offa her."

There was almost a killing but No-britches got O'Neill away from the woman, held him against the wall with one arm and whirled his knout with the other. Spencer let the girl go. But not Lloyd. He held the frantic miner steady under his pistol while McCutcheon called Bugle from the back, told the wide-eyed boy what he had to do.

That was a half-hour ago. Now, they all waited in a shrill and stretching silence, broken only by bottle on glass and O'Neill's phlegmy breathing. Lloyd leaned against the wall at the front, his eyes fixed on O'Neill. He stood quiet, a dangerous calm surrounding him. Andy poured and carried drinks for the two white outlaws. No-britches prowled. Once, when he passed by, Andy saw the deep glow of red flickering in his eyes. The Indian was drunk on the pilfered bottle. Roy Spencer brooded over his drink. His pistol lay at his hand on the counter and at every sound he grabbed it, tensing. A beading of nervous sweat covered his face and he had trouble keeping his lips still. The room was thick with the smell of fear.

Outside, bootheels rapped on the planking in front of the store. A voice called: "McCutcheon. It's me—— Fargo. What's happening in there?"

Spencer swung over the counter to lay his gun alongside McCutcheon's head in a flash. "Tell him it's all right," he hissed. "Tell him!"

"Fargo," Andy called. "It's—everything is all right. Come in. . . ."

His voice squeaked, trailed off. Spencer jabbed his neck with the gun, cursed him in a whisper. There was no answer from outside.

Then: "I'm coming in."

Footsteps near the door. Spencer wheeled away from Andy, crouched with his long pistol aimed full at the door. O'Neill backed to where the opening door would cover him, his gun drawn. No-britches was nowhere to be seen. The latch lifted slowly. No sound, not even breathing. The door came open an inch, another inch.

"Fargo! Don't come in!" Lloyd Dempster moved with his shout, jumped on O'Neill wrapping his strong arms around the man from behind.

"You sonofabitch!" Roy Spencer shrilled.

He fired; fired again. Lloyd's grip slackened. He slid to the floor and Spencer put another shot into him where he lay. At that moment Fargo came through the door. He came through fast and he came through low, crouched and weaving, rifle held ready.

Andy shouted, "Fargo—look out!"

But it was all crazy by then, shots and screams and No-britches' ululating whoops. Spencer and O'Neill both fired at the crouched figure of the Marshal and at the same instant No-britches, yipping like a dog, swung his murderous knout. The rock glanced off Fargo's head and he dropped like a dead man. O'Neill and Spencer's shots burned the air where Fargo had been before the Indian downed him.

O'Neill shouted, "Got him! Let's get out of here!"

Roy Spencer sent his one remaining shot in the general direction of the downed Marshal, ran to the door. No-britches swung his knout against one of the lamps and fire licked the wall as oil splattered.

The three mounted outside, milled around as a spate of firing broke out from up-canyon. *The mine!* Andy thought. They had tried for the gold. Prudhomme had been right to move it. He ignored the fire, ran to the porch and stood looking up the street. A shot kicked splinters into his face. He ducked, backed inside. Roy Spencer and his two, hollering and shooting at shadows, rode off down-canyon.

Right behind them came the other four, riding break-neck in the frozen ruts of the street and firing as they came. McCutcheon recognized the bulky figure of Hobie Spencer, his huge mustache a black slash in the round face. The outlaw saw McCutcheon and fired three shots into the store as he pounded by.

The sudden quiet was a shock. Andy pushed himself off the wall where he'd clung away from Hobie Spencer's bullets. *The fire. He had to put out the fire.* But it had burned itself out, the oil igniting fast and burning quickly. The wall smoldered and smoked but there was no flame.

"Who were they? I want names."

He turned, incredulous. Fargo, a trickle of blood down one cheek, was on his feet. He swayed but he stood.

"You're alive." Andy hurried to him; Fargo pushed

him aside, walked unsteadily to where Lloyd Dempster lay. "It was Roy Spencer. And a man called O'Neill. The Indian is just No-britches. That's the only name he has."

"Which one shot Lloyd?"

"Roy Spencer."

Fargo knelt near the stricken miner, pulled the man's head around. Lloyd's eyelids flickered, opened.

"Take it easy, Welsh." Fargo's voice was gentle.

The eyes focused slowly. Lloyd Dempster managed a small smile when he saw who held him.

"Ah," he said. "The Fargo, is it." He stifled a cough, struggled to speak. "Sometimes a man must stand. . . ."

He coughed and the blood came, staining his lips. Then he was dead.

Fargo stood slowly.

"They never learn. He should have kept his mouth shut and stayed alive."

"He saved your life!" Andy couldn't hold it back. "He saved your stinking life!"

Fargo looked at him as if there was a bad smell about him. He picked up a hat with a crushed crown from the floor, moved to the door. His piercing eyes turned back and rested for a moment on the dead miner.

"What he did, McCutcheon," Fargo said quietly, "was almost *cost* me my life, not save it. And threw his own away in the process. But he was a man."

He shook his head, pulled open the door.

"Fargo, wait. Where you going?"

The big man pulled the hat on gingerly, wincing as it touched where the knout had struck.

"To sea," he said. "'In a beautiful pea green boat.'"

The door slammed behind him.

Gault was a town in turmoil. Within minutes of the Spoilers' departure the street boiled with people. Irate citizens, brave warriors now that the danger had passed, flocked to the store. Foster Prudhomme, mud-covered and drawn, pushed into the crush. He edged around the blanketed figure on the floor, made his way to Andy sitting on the counter.

"They tried for the gold," he said, speaking low. "Shot up the place when they found the safe empty. I was in the mine, stayed there 'til it was over. It was Hobie Spencer."

Andy blew out a sigh. "Roy and that crazy Indian came here. And another one—O'Neill. They were after Fargo. Roy Spencer killed Lloyd."

"Lloyd?" The little Mayor turned slowly. "My God. Has anyone told Nellie?"

"Not yet. She was—upset herself. It was a mess, Foster. A real mess."

"And where was your high-powered marshal while all this was going on? Huh? They ride into town, kill people, frighten those they don't kill. And where's the man we hired to protect us? To keep the peace?"

"Listen, Prudhomme—he was here! He almost died and if it hadn't been for Lloyd he would have."

The mayor grimaced around his prominent teeth. "How many of them did he kill? Humh? Where are the bodies? And where is he now—hiding under his bed?"

Andy flushed, shook his head.

"Well, then," Prudhomme said, "let's go find out."

They hurried in a body to the stone jail. McCutcheon was aware as he pushed through the frozen mud and packed snow that Bugle clung to his hand, going along. He shouldn't be there but Andy was too tired, too confused to send him back home.

There was no one at all in the jail building. They got a lamp lit and looked around, twenty or more crowding into the place.

"He's not here. He's gone!"

A murmur of protest arose and Andy tried to shout it down but to no avail. A stir at the door drew attention and there was Silesia Bragg, wet to the waist from wading the creek. She pushed through to McCutcheon and the mayor.

"Where is he? Is he all right?"

"I'll tell you where he is, Mrs. Bragg—your friend Fargo. He's halfway to Freemantle by now and not looking back."

"You don't know that," Andy said, but it sounded weak even to him.

"It ain't so!" a treble voice shouted. "It ain't!"

"You shut up, boy. Now, look here Mrs. Bragg. You see what a mess we're in. And your foundling, our sworn—*and paid*—protector is running like a fat rabbit from a starving wolf."

Silesia said, "Why don't *you* shut up, Foster. 'Til you know what you're talkin' about." She pulled Bugle through the circle of grumbling adults. "Bugle—do you know where he is?"

"Sure, I know. He went to the lower camp, that's where."

A sudden silence settled over the room. Andy moved to his son, knelt before him. The boy's face was tear-streaked.

"Listen, son. Did you see Marshal Fargo? Did he tell you he was going to the camp?"

Bugle shook his head back and forth; a groan went up.

"But he is," the boy shouted, twisting in his grasp. "I know he is!"

Silesia's firm voice settled the crowd. "How do you know, Bugle? Is it because you think Fargo ain't the kind of man to run away?"

He nodded, said quickly, "But that ain't all. Look —" He pointed to the gun rack by the door; all eyes swiveled to it. "You see? He took the Sharps and the Henry, too. He just wouldn't carry all that 'less he figured on doin' some shootin'."

Foster Prudhomme looked from the earnest lad, to

the depleted gun rack, back again. He closed his eyes and Andy noticed bluish circles under them.

"Boys," the little Mayor said softly, "what is it the book says? 'And a little child shall lead them.' . . ."

Chapter 7

THERE WERE JUST two solid buildings in the lower camp, the saloon and a longhouse next door where the cribs were. Fargo had seen them in daylight that morning on his solitary scout. Now, clinging to a rock outcropping halfway up the side of the canyon, he looked again. Carefully, pushing his head up slow. No need to take chances. Hobie Spencer might be good enough to make some of his discipline—dodging hardacres stand sentry duty. There was no one in sight, though. Lights in the two log buildings, smoke from some of the soddies and shacks. Over the liquid sound of the creek he heard music. A piano in the saloon. Big chords and long intricate runs. Fargo knew little about music but he thought the piano was being well played. Well, the performance would be short tonight.

He rolled back behind his rock. The wind had cleared some of the exposed ridges of snow, so his vantage was dry. He pulled the Sharps rifle to him, checked the action, loaded it. He wedged it between two rocks where it would be safe until he needed it. He had no doubt that he would need it—suddenly and badly. There were twenty, thirty men down there and he was alone. One man with a dull throb in his head and muscles creaking with weariness.

No good to think about it. Fargo stuffed a full load into the Henry, checked his Colt and buttoned the coat over it. His breath puffed white, the vapor dissolving in the wind. He sniffed, testing the breeze. South wind.

Still cold but with some of the warm desert in it. It wouldn't be long before the chinooks came, loosening the grip of winter. Then the pass would open and people would come. Sooner or later one of them would be Charlie Ward.

He pushed the thought aside, rolled around the outcropping and started down into the Spoiler's camp.

It took him fifteen minutes to get close, moving from cover to cover. He had to move slow; men kept going from one building to the other. Finally, he made it to the door of a stable attached to the side of the saloon nearest the creek. He slipped inside, rifle ready. The stable stank. There were ten horses tied along one side. Some still saddled. The place hadn't been mucked out for a long time. Fargo checked the whole thing quickly, soothing the animals with clucks and pats. He had the place to himself.

The inside stable-wall was also the saloon's wall. He looked for cracks, found several but none good enough. The piano was loud, now. Almost as loud as the stable's smell. Fargo got a hoof rasp from a clutter of horse-shoeing tools. In minutes he had dug the chinking from between two logs, giving him a hole to look through.

It was a big room he looked into, rough and badly lit. A long bar, with a faded blonde woman behind it, poker tables and drinking tables. The piano stood against the far wall and a wide man with a moon face and black mustache was playing. He had fingers like sausages but they were sure and deft on the keys. The Indian, No-britches, hunkered near the piano, a bottle in his hand, his strange weapon laid out before him. The room was murky with smoke and loud with talk, harsh laughter and the overpowering thunder of the piano.

"Hobie. Hobie, listen. . . ." A thin man with eyes that looked half-closed moved into view and Fargo recognized him as one of the men in the trouble at McCutcheon's. The thin man moved to the piano player, put a hand on one massive shoulder and said something that Fargo could not catch. The music stopped on a discord, the wide man turning to face the other.

"My own brother—and a premier fool." The voice was cultured, soft, with a muted Southern quality in it.

"Now, Hobie," Roy Spencer said. "I just said O'Neill wants to go back for that miner's woman. Why not? The Mole won't need her no more."

He laughed and another man joined in—a short, bearded man, very drunk.

"Shut up!" Hobie Spencer's voice cut through the smoke, silencing the room. "O'Neill is dangerous in his stupidity. But I expect it from him. Not from you."

The younger Spencer shuffled his feet, looked down.

The bearded drunk said, "Just a minute. How come you call me stupid, huh? We did our job, didn't we? We got that—that Fargo, the marshal. What'd you get, Hobie? Humh—what? Where's all that gold?"

The bearded man stopped his tirade abruptly as Hobie Spencer spun slowly away from the piano and stood. Spencer's shoulders were huge and bunched with muscle; his stomach bulged hard and firm. The man had the dense appearance of marble. He moved through a perfect silence to the drunken O'Neill near the bar. Hobie made no threatening gesture, just stood, arms dangling, a faint smile under the black mustache. O'Neill's color faded and the pockmarks stood out in contrast.

"So," Hobie Spencer said, "the mangy little cur can bark. Can it also bite?"

"I don't want no trouble, Hobie."

"That's admirable, O'Neill. Laudable. Consider—— he wants no trouble, this despicable pig! This foul-mouthed idiot who molests pregnant women."

O'Neill started to say something and Spencer hissed sharply between his teeth. O'Neill shut his mouth.

"Even fools deserve explanations from their commander and you shall have yours." It was obvious the wide man was addressing the rest of the men more than the unfortunate O'Neill. "It's true that I made a miscalculation. I underestimated someone up there, in Gault. Perhaps this Fargo we've heard so much about since he gunned Sudden Jack. No matter. Someone had the foresight to move the gold and we missed it. This time. We shall not miss it again."

The men cheered. Spencer waited, eyes pinning the bearded man until it became quiet.

"What you did, you simpleton, was come within a whisker of giving those mice in Gault an issue to rally around. So long as they argue, so long as they bicker and cavil we can do what we like. But let them think they are avenging outraged womanhood and you have unified them. And with a cause, even mice become dangerous. You understand?"

The man nodded, eyes shifting, darting.

"Fine." Spencer smiled coldly. "Now, tell the assembled brethren what you are, O'Neill—and we'll call the lecture over for this time."

"Hobie, please. . . ."

"Tell them!"

O'Neill's eyes dropped; his harsh voice was only a whisper. "A——a mangy cur."

"What else?"

"A simpleton, I guess."

Spencer nodded. "Exactly. Now have a drink and don't try to think——you have decidedly inferior equipment for that activity. Savannah——drinks all around. We'll have a wake for the town of Gault. Drink up!"

The men crowded to the bar, chattering. Spencer went back to the piano, sat looking at the keys. The huge hands settled slowly on the keyboard, seeming to flow with a sinuous grace nothing so blunt should have.

Fargo pulled away from his peek-hole as the music began. He had seen and marked the men responsible for Lloyd's death. And he had discovered that Hobie Spencer was not a man to be taken lightly.

The saloon sat next to the creek, the front facing the canyon side where it stretched up to the sloping rim. The space before the porch was churned to muddy white, frozen now. Fargo checked his escape route, noted the nearest cover. Satisfied, he opened his coat and jumped up onto the porch. The piano started again. He cocked the Henry, opened the door and stepped inside.

Somebody said, "Hey!"

The piano stopped. There wasn't a sound. The room was all frozen faces, caught in time, all looking toward the doorway.

"My name is Fargo," he said into the silence—and started firing.

He triggered the Henry deliberately at first, picking targets. His first shot smashed O'Neill's chest. He fired at Roy Spencer diving behind the bar and immediately swiveled back to Hobie, off the piano stool and lifting a pistol. Fargo fired and Hobie Spencer fell. A bullet zinged into the wood at his head and he squeezed a shot at the flash.

Men were jumping, diving, scrambling in all directions. The woman had disappeared. Thick smoke from the rifle mixed with the rest and made it hard to see. Fargo crouched in the doorway, cursing out loud and pumping shot after shot into the bedlam. The Indian slid out from behind the piano, moving like a puma. A chilling sound came from his open mouth and he swung the knout around his head.

Fargo continued to pull the trigger. The Henry clicked empty and there was no time to reload, no time for anything as the screaming No-britches covered the last few feet in a rush. His eyes blazed red in triumph. He started the killing blow with his knout, leaning his body into it. Fargo dipped to one knee, reversing the rifle, swinging it like an axe. He hit the Indian across the chest, the stock shattering against his shoulder. The swinging knout thudded against the wall and No-britches crumpled like a broken doll.

Fargo threw aside the useless rifle, pulled his Colt. A shot blazed from behind the bar. He fired twice in return. Hobie moved on the floor and Fargo shot at him again before jumping out into the covering dark.

He reached the outcropping without being followed and dropped gratefully to the ground. His breath whistled in his chest and little dots swam in his vision. He reached out a hand blindly and found the Sharps where he'd left it. He pulled it to him, laid his face on the cool barrel. He was tired, awful goddam tired. He hadn't near got his strength back from the weeks in the mountains, the wound.

"Any sign, Dan?" The words came clearly, carrying in the thin air. Dan said there was no sign and then several voices mixed together.

Fargo stared straight up at the high, cold stars. Men were moving around down at the saloon. He could hear them. Out of the excited chatter, he figured out that in his attack, he had killed O'Neill and somebody named Winkle, whoever he was. No-britches was still unconscious and Hobie Spencer was hurt, nobody knew how bad. Fargo ran a hand over his face, felt the grim lines there. No time to be tired. Not yet. He rolled over and pushed his head up over the rock.

Two men with rifles were circling the clearing. More men clustered near the saloon's door, the light from inside throwing weird shadows on the muddy snow. A thin figure moved into the doorway, blocking the light.

"Some of you get up the side of the canyon, find his trail."

Nobody answered and nobody moved.

"You hear me?" Roy Spencer said. "Get after that sonofabitch!"

"In the dark?" It was a heavy voice, slow and deep. "Go after that fella? You go to hell, Spencer."

"Listen," Roy said. "He killed Winkle and O'Neill —wounded my brother. You gonna let him get away with that?"

"Damn right," the heavy voice said. "I wouldn't

care if he shot Robert E. Lee—he's too much for me and I know it. I'm goin' to bed."

There was a chorus of assent and the group broke up despite Roy Spencer's protests. Fargo slid the Sharps into position, squinted over the sights. Couldn't see Roy for the roof. He waited.

"Wait a minute," Roy Spencer said. "One of you get some water for Hobie. You there—you hear me?"

There was no answer. All of the men had melted into the shadows except for the two with rifles continuing their slow search. Spencer cursed high and wild. In a moment, he came out with a bucket and ran to the creek. Fargo rose, braced a knee on the rock and brought the heavy Buffalo gun to his shoulder. It was a long shot for a Sharps.

"Spencer!" Fargo's voice cracked through the canyon.

Roy stiffened, bucket dangling, and turned slowly. One of the riflemen fired. Fargo steadied in his brace. Very clearly he saw Roy Spencer's hanging jaw, a dark stain of some kind on his shirt. He took up trigger slack slow and easy. The Sharps boomed and Spencer was slapped with a giant hand, halfway across the creek. Fargo ducked.

Sometimes a man must stand

Must stand, must stand, must stand. He rolled away and wormed upward toward the rim. . . .

Chapter 8

"SO IT'S STARTED. The slaughter and the crying— God's creatures tearing at each other's throats and no mercy anywhere."

McCutcheon lowered his head over his plate and said nothing. As she talked, his wife slid golden slabs of fried mush onto his platter. Across the table his son jittered on his seat, pushing his food around but unable to eat. His eyes followed his mother's upright figure warily.

"Four men dead. Only the beginning, Mr. McCutcheon. This killer Fargo, where will he stop? Where? And who will forget that my husband was responsible for all of it. Examine your conscience, Mr. McCutcheon."

"Crimey, Ma," Bugle burst out, "they come up here and just shot ol' Lloyd. No tellin' who'da been next. I'm glad Fargo killed 'em!"

Caroline's thin lips peeled back from her teeth. "Andrew! Get down on your knees—right now!—and pray sweet Jesus for forgiveness. Pray, son."

"Ah, Ma. . . ."

"On your knees!"

McCutcheon stared at his food, congealing on the plate. He heard Bugle slide off his chair, begin to mumble.

McCutcheon said, "Caroline, listen to me. Now, just wait before you start throwin' Scripture at me. I got Fargo hired, that's right. And I did it because this town was desperate. You know it better'n I do, much as you talked about not being safe in your own home. Well, now we got somebody'll make them rowdies think before they come up here shootin' off guns and like that. Did you know they tried to steal the gold? Did you? And if it hadn't been for—"

"I know that the cure may be worse than the disease, Mr. McCutcheon. I do know that. Vengeance is mine saith the Lord and a taste for blood is abomination in His eyes." Her voice softened. "All right, Andrew. Go on to school."

Bugle scuttled out with a bare 'goodbye.' He'd head straight for the jail, Andy knew, to see his hero, Fargo. His stomach burned. He pushed back his chair.

"Opening the store with no breakfast, Mr. McCutcheon? You'll surely sicken."

He shook his head, wordless. Caroline moved to him and laid a hand on his chest, gently. Her eyes were clear. She was so sure, so certain.

"Look into your heart, husband. There is evil around us. But we don't have to feed that evil; let it feed upon itself. The Lord works in mysterious ways His wonders to perform. Send that man from our midst while your soul is still your own."

He took her hand pressed it to his lips. The fingers were cold. He got his coat and hat and went out the side door into the bright morning. He stood for a moment, enjoying the sun's early warmth, the crisp air. Water dripped from the eaves; the snow was slowly melting.

"Where are you going?"

Caroline stood in the doorway. Her brow was creased and the lips had all but disappeared.

"We're burying Lloyd Dempster, Caroline. Two children and another one coming soon." He breathed deep, looked up at the cloudless sky. "Doesn't the book say—an eye for an eye, a tooth for a tooth?"

"It says that, Mr. McCutcheon." He looked at her; her face was serene. "It does *not* say—three eyes for an eye. Or four, or ten."

The door closed gently.

Foster Prudhomme came while Fargo was shaving. He'd slept like the dead, an exhausted, dreamless coma which had left him vague and grouchy.

"Marshal Fargo," the little man said, "Gault is in your debt. You can't know how it feels to have a competent lawman."

Fargo turned and looked at the little man. He seemed serious. He wore a plum-colored suit and a black foulard. His usual hard hat sat squarely on his head.

"Glad you're satisfied." He turned back to the mirror.

"More than, Mr. Fargo. Much more than. That was

a brave thing you did. Invading their camp and shooting down those—"

"Just a minute." He walked to the mayor, looked down at him. Prudhomme's eyes widened. "That's enough. I don't like myself much this morning. Or this town. When McCutcheon got me appointed marshal you bucked. Now, you're happy because your precious gold is safe. Yes, Mr. Mayor, I know about that."

"You can't think the gold is my prime concern."

"I don't know what I think. Except right now I'm ready to admit the almighty made a mistake when he dreamed up people." Fargo walked to the window, looked out. "Is everyone as happy with me as you, Prudhomme?"

After a moment, the mayor said, "Well, Fargo— generally they are. Generally. But it doesn't matter. You're needed and I think you know that. You're a man of sensibilities—despite the war and everything you've seen and done. Right now you feel the weight of those men you killed. As you should." Prudhomme walked to the gun rack, fingered the weapons. He turned and a strange dignity touched him. "If it's any comfort, Gault would have surely died without you these last few days. It still could."

"I don't think it's that bad."

"You know it is, Marshal. Better than any of us. They want the gold. They'll be back. If I can help, call on me. That's what I came to say. And I'm sorry we missed you at the funeral."

"Funeral?"

"We buried Lloyd Dempster this morning. Mrs. Bragg—Silesia, she tried to wake you. I guess you were too tired."

It was an odd experience walking through the town that day. People spoke, congratulated him—but at the same time there was a withdrawal that he could feel. Like they were afraid of him. Fargo wondered how professional killers ever could be sure any offer of friendship was not simply fear. Probably they couldn't. Probably they all were lonely, beyond the pale and knowing it. Maybe he'd find out before this was done. He pushed mechanically through the mud, not feeling the warming sun. People were flighty, that's all. One day this, next day that—and it had nothing to do with morals, abstracts and all of those things.

He had no trouble finding the Dempster house. It was a shack like the rest but it was the only one with black crepe fluttering on the door. Smoke drifted from a blackened stone chimney. Near the door, a wooden sled leaned against the wall. It was roughly fashioned and Fargo knew Lloyd had made it for one of his children. He knocked gently.

Silesia Bragg opened the door. She wore a dress and it made her softer, more feminine. Her hair was a dark cloud brushed shining and let hang around her shoulders. She smiled and her eyes said warm things to him.

"I told Nellie you'd come."

The house was small and very clean. Nellie Dempster, two little towheads clinging to her skirts, greeted him. She wore black and her eyes were red-rimmed and swollen. A pretty woman, her stomach distended in pregnancy.

"You're Fargo." She took both his hands, looked up into his face. "Lloyd thought much of you."

"My sympathies, Mrs. Dempster."

The girl's eyes looked straight into his. "Listen—whatever the vultures say, whatever anyone tries to make of it—you did right to punish those men. You did right!"

Her eyes filled slowly and she squeezed his hands, turned away. Silesia spoke from beside the table: "Coffee, Fargo?"

He sat, took the steaming cup and kept his eyes away from Nellie. He heard her take the two children into the other room, shut the door. Silesia's hand rested on his shoulder.

"A sad day," he said.

"Young death is always sad." Her hand turned his face up to her. "I was afraid for you."

"Killers never get hurt. Don't you know that?" It was harsh and he knew it but something was pushing at him this day. Something deep and ugly. Silesia pulled away slowly, took the coffee pot back to the fire and hung it. He said, "Mrs. Dempster—she's very brave, isn't she?"

Silesia sat across from him; her expression was carefully controlled. "What else can she be?"

"I mean—two kids, another coming. Losing her husband. She's taking it well."

"She's taking it. That's the only choice she has."

"I forgot, Silesia. You've been through it."

"Everyone has. Oh, Fargo, don't let it eat at you. Stay away from it! You're a man. A complete man. Don't get involved or you'll be weak when you oughta be strong. Don't get close to the people!"

Her hands were clenched on the table and her fine eyes were cloudy with feeling.

"Including you, Silesia?"

"Yes!" She burst out. "You took on a job. I wish you hadn't but you did. A stinkin' job, but one that has to be done. You're the only man there is to do it. Then *do it*, Fargo!"

A tear ran down her cheek. He stood abruptly, walked to her. With a finger he touched the wet streak on her face.

"I never thought I'd see you cry."

She smiled sadly. "I save my tears for them that's living."

Later, walking outside, he felt the sun, smelled the air. It was good.

The Gault town council was in extraordinary session —and the most extraordinary thing was that they hadn't begun to shout after a full hour. Because, McCutcheon admitted to himself, Foster Prudhomme wouldn't argue. He'd been sitting back, listening as

McCutcheon and the other three discussed what to do about Fargo. Tucker, the assayer, would vote with Prudhomme, no matter what. That left King, the livery owner and Shakey Burger, the barber.

Kunz was saying, ". . . . and so now you want to fire him. Is that right? I don't understand, Andy."

Foster Prudhomme smiled, pushed his lips back and forth over his prominent teeth.

"Listen," McCutcheon said. "I sponsored him—yes. But now I have doubts. He killed four men. Four! Do you know what blood lust is? And not only the killing, the way he did it. Just—blazin' away."

"There was fifteen, twenty of them. What else could he do?"

"I don't know! I just know all this death and violence, it ain't right. It's against the—against nature. I say what we got is a cure that's worse than the disease!"

Prudhomme's eyes cut toward him. "That's the second time you've said that."

"Well, it could be true."

"Yes, and it could also be true that Gault would be a ghost town today if it hadn't been for Marshal Fargo! *Your* Marshal Fargo. This is silly."

McCutcheon felt the flush creeping up his neck. "All right. But the problem is solved now, ain't it? McCall, Roy Spencer, O'Neill—all dead. Hobie laid up. It's been three days and we ain't heard a peep from the lower camp. There's nothin' left to be afraid of. The killer has done his work. What do we need with him now?" He looked around. "There's one thing I didn't tell anyone. Fargo shot Sudden Jack McCall in the back."

Kunz and Burger were shocked. Tucker frowned and looked to Prudhomme. The mayor bit a stogie, lit it with a flaring lucifer.

"So, you see," McCutcheon pressed. "How do we know this man won't go berserk? How do we know the taste of blood ain't gettin' sweeter and sweeter to him?

He's a bigger danger than the Spoilers, I say. Let's vote!"

There was a murmur and McCutcheon knew he had won. They would oust Fargo. He waited for the familiar trill of triumph inside but it didn't come. He was curiously empty.

Prudhomme said, "Just a minute. I'm chairing this meeting. I'll call for votes, if and when." He raised his voice: "Marshal. Come on in here."

The door in the wooden wall of the office opened and Fargo stepped in. His hat shadowed his face but they could see the lines, deep and hard. McCutcheon felt a chill.

"You hear all this?" Prudhomme asked.

"I heard."

Burger said nervously, "Marshal, no offense, but Andy said—I mean, about Jack McCall. . . ."

"What about McCall? That I shot him in the back? I did. Friend Andy didn't tell you how it happened, but then maybe details don't matter—unless they support your cause. Ask him how come he wrapped a blanket around McCall, hid the wound, didn't tell anyone about it."

"Because we needed someone—fast." McCutcheon stood. "This is my home."

"You're a nice man, I can see that. Hide the truth when it suits you. Then lie to make up for the first mistake."

"I didn't lie!"

"You did! By not telling it all. Did you say McCall had two shots at me? Did you tell them I had one shell in my pistol—one!—and McCall spun around just as I fired it? And why he turned, did you tell them that? To put a bullet in your guts! I should have let him do it."

Fargo advanced into the room. He looked at McCutcheon. "Sit down, Andy. I don't know what's chewing on you and I don't even care. What I did last night had to be done. Let 'em get away with a full-scale raid like that and the town's finished. You know that."

"But shootin' into a crowded room!"

"My methods are my own! And your information's bad, anyhow. What did you want me to do—walk in and say please come along you killers, you're under arrest? By myself?" Fargo leveled a finger at them all. "I tell you now—you'll see no such silliness from me. No shoot-outs on main street, no even breaks for a man trying his best to kill me. No. The game I play is hard and if you come in second, you're dead."

McCutcheon sat, fascinated by the animal force of this man, the certainty. The others were as spellbound. There was no sound. Fargo brooded out the window. Then he turned.

"Dead men make poor marshals. Trouble with all of you is you want to treat this feud with the lower camp as a sort of—oh, little routine problem. It's not. It's war. The gold is still here. They know it. Hobie Spencer has twenty or thirty men and he'll rally them when his wounds heal. They'll come. Who's going to stop them, Andy—you?"

"I'm—I'm not a fighter."

Fargo's eyes held on him. "Neither was Lloyd Dempster."

McCutcheon dropped his gaze; he wanted to say something, wipe out that accusation. His mind was shriveled, blank.

"So y'all go on and have your vote or whatever it is you think you got to do. Won't mean nothing. Not to me. I don't rightly know how I got into this thing. But I did. And I'm staying in. When Spencer comes, I'll be here—and it don't have much at all to do with you, McCutcheon and your two-bit store. Or Prudhomme's gold, or the goddam mine." Fargo cracked his knuckles loudly; he shook his head. "Down there is a couple towheaded kids, a strong, good woman—a lot of good people just trying to do right and get along. Somebody has to keep the wolves off 'em. You won't. So you can't fire me, see—I won't let you."

He started for the door.

"Wait," McCutcheon said. "All right—let's say we need you and we already owe you thanks. But you've got to stop this—this killing!"

"What the hell do you care, McCutcheon," Fargo said. "You got plenty blankets. . . ."

Chapter 9

CHARLIE WARD rode into the lower camp at dusk. Not much of a place. But small enough so that if Fargo was here he'd have no trouble finding him. Charlie thought about that a minute, then dismounted and led his two animals into the shadow of a large soddy. They were beat. The trip through the snow-choked pass had been rough. Charlie's ginger beard had sprouted and his face was red and cracked from cold and exposure. He was tired, too. And that, Charlie knew, was no condition to be in looking for a man like Fargo.

Not much activity for a gold camp. He could see light and some traffic near the saloon. The building beside it was lighted. But everything else was dead. Smoke from soddies, cracks shooting light spears from some shacks. That's all. The door of the nearest soddy opened and Charlie stepped back as two men came out. The men were rough-dressed and bearded. They didn't notice him in the shadow.

"Gonna be full moon," one said. "Reckon Hobie figures on goin' up to Gault tonight and givin' them fools a lesson?"

"He will, don't worry. But he ain't up to ridin' just yet with that nick he got. That marshal must be crazy. . . ."

They were walking away toward the saloon and Charlie tried to catch as much of the conversation as he could, edging around the soddy, leaving his horses. He trailed the two, keeping to the shadows.

"He'll think crazy," the first man said, "time we hit that town like Jeb Stuart's cavalry and stuff his bad ass down a mine shaft! Come on—I'll buy the first one."

They stomped onto the porch of the saloon and inside. Charlie stood for a moment in the deepening dark. So this wasn't Gault. But that was no guarantee that Fargo wasn't here anyway, whatever it was. Some trouble between a man named Hobie and the Marshal of Gault. No concern of his. Unless. . . . He considered it. It just might be that trouble could help him. Sounded like this Hobie somebody meant to make a real, ride-'em-down raid. And if Fargo was in Gault maybe, just maybe, Charlie could slip up on him in the confusion. He knew Fargo better than anyone alive. And he had no desire to face him on even terms if he could avoid it. This might be the way.

Charlie unbuttoned his heavy mackinaw, removed his gloves. He got his pistol—a Navy Colt like the one Fargo had taken with him from Fort Denman—out of its holster, stuck it into the coat pocket. He kept his hand in there with it. Somebody was tinkling on a piano inside, barely heard over the noise of the creek. Charlie moved to the door, pushed it open and stepped in quickly, slid to one side with his back against the wall.

Somebody said, "What the hell!" and it got quiet.

The piano stopped. A wide man with a moon face had been playing it with one hand. The other was bandaged. Charlie saw this in his first rapid survey of the room. He was looking for Fargo and when he didn't see him, he relaxed some. He was the focus of attention, all right. About fifteen men were scattered about the room. One was a tall Indian with the whole seat cut out of his strides. There was a woman behind the rough bar and she broke the silence.

"Hello, there." Her voice was whiskey-burred. "You come through the pass, for Crissake?"

He nodded, walked to the bar. "And a damn cold job it was. Whiskey if you please, Ma'm."

Nobody else moved. Nobody spoke. Charlie could feel the hostility and hair rippled on the back of his neck. He turned sideways to the bar, wedged his left elbow up on it and leaned. The right hand gripped the Colt in his pocket.

"You must want to get to Gault real bad, Mister— makin' the pass when the snow's down."

The woman poured a generous drink, left the bottle. Charlie picked up the glass, his eyes fixed on the man at the piano. He just sat there, rubbing a black mustache with his good hand, looking up at the ceiling. Charlie downed the drink. He poured another. Still nobody moved.

"I'm looking for a man," Charlie said.

The woman shot a glance toward the piano. "You the law, Mister?"

He laughed. "Not hardly, Ma'm. Private thing. I'm gonna kill this man when I find him."

There was a small stir. The moon-faced man was looking at him now.

"This fella you want," the woman asked, "he got a name? Some of these men here, they work up to Gault now and again. Maybe they could tell you if he's there —your friend."

Charlie turned a little more into the room. The hand in his pocket was slippery on the gunbutt.

"He ain't hard to notice and that's a fact. Big fella —wide in the shoulder. Kind of hard-faced with black hair, and the kind of eyes seem to hit out at you, like. . . ."

Everybody in the room sucked a breath at the same time. Charlie tensed; he'd hit something. What, he didn't know—but something.

"Savannah." It was the man at the piano. "The gentleman's drinks are on me and I'd be honored if he'd join me."

The faded blonde woman pushed Charlie's money back at him, nodded toward the wide man. "That there's Hobie Spencer, Mister. You heard what he said."

Spencer rose to his feet as Charlie walked to the table. He was a solid man. He had a round belly, huge shoulders and hands like hams. He bowed and indicated a chair. Charlie turned the chair around so that he would be facing the room, then sat. He saw an approving glint in Hobie Spencer's clear eyes as he resumed his own seat.

"So," he said softly, "you are going to kill Fargo."

He's here, Charlie thought, Fargo is here. Best go very slow. He turned sideways to the table, removed his wide-brimmed hat and placed it in his lap.

"I mentioned no name," he said.

Spencer's hard, shining cheeks tightened. "Advice, my nameless friend. For no cost. Do not, I beg you, make sport or play me for the fool. It would be a most expensive indulgence, sir. These men are mine. This camp, mean, ragged and filthy though it be, is also mine. You leave—or you stay, entirely at my whim." A slow smile grew under the slash of mustache; he managed a bow without rising. "Hobart Remington Spencer, Third. At your service, sir. . . ."

Charlie jerked his head in answer. "Denman. Charlie Denman. And if you're the he-mule in this here lash-up, why I'd be obliged if you'd send someone to care for my animals. Down the road a ways."

Spencer's smile spread; he motioned to one of the idlers, sent him to bring Charlie's stock to the saloon's stable. The place loosened up, then. Bottles clinked and cards slapped. Charlie picked up his drink, feeling the warmth of the first two he'd had.

"Might be, Mr. Spencer, we could do each other a turn."

A scream erupted from the room's rear. It was a

terrible sound, ripped out of a vibrating throat. The Indian with the cutaway trousers shuffled slowly to the center of the room. A weird, guttural chant came from him. Some sort of rawhide mace dangled from one wrist as he shuffled and circled. Men scrambled to give him room. His bronze face was slicked with sweat and his eyes were inflamed.

"That's No-britches," Spencer said. "He's drunk and his pride is hurt. Very bad thing. Your friend, Fargo, bested him hand to hand and poor No-britches' Indian soul is in torment. I sincerely hope he doesn't kill anyone."

The Indian shuffled in wider circles. A chair hit his foot and he whirled like a panther, the mace whistling through a short arc. It struck the heavy chair and demolished it. No-britches laughed; high, barking laughter—like a wolf's blood-yip. Everyone gave him room. Several of the men laid hands openly on gunbutts. The man must be dangerous.

"Drink, Chief," Savannah said, wheedling. "Come get the pretty whiskey."

But the Indian was beyond drinking, now. He shuffled to his open-mouthed chant, going faster and faster. He passed Charlie and his red-lit eyes fastened on him. He stopped. Spencer leaned back with a wicked smile. The Indian swayed, eyes fixed on Charlie. He slid a foot forward, swung his weapon in a blurred circle. Charlie did not move. The mace thumped the floor six inches from his boot. No-britches, silent now, slid his foot forward a little more.

Spencer spoke softly. "What do you think of our tame Indian?"

"I think," Charlie said evenly, "if he moves that foot again, I'll kill him."

He lifted the hat from his lap uncovering the Colt, rock-steady and cocked, and pointed straight at the Indian's belly.

No-britches stood immobile. He was drunk but he wasn't stupid; the foot did not move. Spencer nodded to one of the men behind the Indian and he stepped forward, slashed a gun barrel hard to the side of No-britches' head. No-britches fell face forward, his naked buttocks quivered, went slack. He was out, snoring softly.

"Very neat," Hobie Spencer said. Two men dragged the drunken Indian out the door. "Good—that thing with the hat. You're a careful man."

Charlie holstered the Colt, rubbed a hand over his brow, suddenly wet with sweat. "Not careful, Spencer. Scared. That Injun's dangerous."

"He is. They put him in the white man's army a year or two ago. Took his knout away, wouldn't let him drink. Made him wear trousers, which—as you saw—he despises. He wound up in the stockade, of course. Had no idea what was going on. He made a knout—like the one you saw—and one night he left, killing five soldiers on the way. Yes—a dangerous man. But not, I suspect, nearly as dangerous as our mutual enemy, Marshal Fargo."

Charlie couldn't hide the start. "Marshal!"

"Ah. A piece of information you did not have. Yes, he is legally town marshal of Gault. Which somewhat complicates your mission, does it not?"

"But how could he be? He's a deserter! He faces a firing squad if they get him back."

Spencer's look was suddenly appraising. Charlie stopped. His honest indignation was not what Spencer wanted to hear.

"I'm not sure," the wide man said slowly, "that applies, sir. Not here. Half the men in this camp are deserters from one army or another. Myself—late of the Richmond Zouaves, captain of scouts and separated without benefit of messy and time-wasting administrative niceties." His wide-set eyes brooded on Charlie for a moment. "However, it may make some small difference to the good people of Gault. I understand there is feeling against Marshal Fargo in the town. Perhaps we can feed that feeling with this information."

"Feeling against him—for what?"

Spencer's face got hard and smooth, like polished ivory. "For invading us, here, alone. For killing my stupid brother and two others, wounding me. Naturally, the idiots up there can't see what a superb instrument they have acquired. All they see is the blood and not the effect, the violence and not the necessity for it."

"He's a hard man, Spencer. He don't quit. Not never. If Fargo's bought into your game you better go real slow—and dig a lot of graves. He just don't give up."

"I thought not. Tell me about him. Everyone has a weakness. Even Achilles, despite his mother's superhuman efforts to the contrary. What is Fargo's weakness?"

Charlie spoke carefully, thinking about what he said. "I've known him right on to six years. Best soldier I ever saw. Bar none—and I mean *none*. He has a—a thing, a feeling like, about what to do when things get tight. You know what I mean? When there's a threat or danger. Other people have to think about what to do—Fargo, he just *knows!*"

"A natural antagonist. An atavism. I tell you, sir, I am not anxious to face him again. Yet I must. And soon. . . ."

He turned to the piano, his bandaged left hand remaining on the table. There was a crusted bullet furrow above his left ear. Spencer's right hand ran expertly over the keys, then stumbled. The huge hand slammed the keyboard. The sound jangled in the suddenly silent room.

Hobie Spencer's wide face twisted. He held the bandaged left hand up, elbow propped on the table. He stared at it. Charlie stared too, caught by the drama of the man's actions. Slowly the hand lowered to the tabletop and Charlie saw the big black gun in Spencer's right hand, leveled at him steadily, hammer at full cock.

"Now," Spencer said softly, "we talk, friend Charlie. Put both of your tricky hands flat on the table and do not breathe too loud."

Charlie did as he was told, chest tight.

"You smell like authority, sir. Convince me otherwise or make your peace with whatever God you fancy."

"You're wrong. All I want is Fargo dead—and I don't care how. I swear that's true!"

"Your oaths interest me not at all, Denman. If that's your name. You are not convincing me."

The knuckles of his gun-hand began to whiten.

Charlie yelled, "Wait! Inside pocket—my discharge. I got nothing to do with the army, with anybody!"

Spencer had the woman get the paper, spread it before him. He glanced at it but his attention did not waver from Charlie and neither did the gun.

"Well. The name is Ward, we see. Late of 8th Missouri Cavalry—Fort Denman. Of course. Sergeant, six years service. Excellent record—battles, wounds. All right, Sergeant, now tell me why you must kill this Fargo. And make no mistake—" The wide face was smooth, placid—"you are talking for your life. Why do you want him dead?"

Why? Could he tell this man—or any man—why hate for Fargo choked him like a bile? Could he make him see the years of always being less than Fargo, his friend, his comrade—accepting his strength until his own was a dried up kernel of fear? Tell him of the times Fargo had saved his life, saved him from courtmartial, saved him, saved him, saved him! Until the final time when there was nothing left in Charlie Ward and he'd run, blind, sick with panic and Fargo had saved him again by not leaving 'til last and they'd caught him and charged him with cowardice and Charlie was safe again!

"I'm waiting, Ward."

Charlie focused on the deadly man across the table. He had no doubt Spencer would shoot. He couldn't tell him—or anybody—all there was between Fargo and himself. But he had to tell him something. And it had better be good.

"Fargo," Charlie said, "was in the guardhouse at Denman. Charged with desertion in the face of the enemy in time of war. If he went to trial—I knew, he would tell what really happened that day at Wheeler's Hill. He'd have to, you see—or just let them shoot him and Fargo wouldn't do that. And if he talked, *I* would be where Fargo was. I'd be looking out at that post, watching a firing squad practice for me!"

He lifted a hand to his face, forgetting the threat of the gun, caught up in saying the things he'd locked away so long.

"Go on, Sergeant."

"Night before his general court I was Sergeant of the Guard. I faked a blow on the head, gave Fargo my pistol and turned him free. And then–" He dropped his head to his hands and his voice dropped to a whisper– "I shot him from behind when he ran. . . ."

Spencer made a sound in his throat.

Charlie's head came up. "I meant to kill him! To shut him up, don't you see? I should have killed him! I don't know how he got away! I–"

He shook his head. Hobie Spencer lowered the hammer on his pistol, put it away.

"Sergeant Ward, I think we should form an alliance, you and I. You have convinced me. You turned Fargo loose, your friend, your comrade. Then you shot him in the back. In truth, the whole world is not big enough to hide you."

"As long as he's alive."

Spencer nodded, smiled. "Exactly. Welcome friend Charlie. You are worthy of our company. You are, indeed. . . ."

Chapter 10

"I DON'T WANT approval, McCutcheon. Just an answer. Do you have ten repeating rifles and loads for 'em?"

Fargo leaned on the counter, kept his eyes on the storekeeper. McCutcheon's paunch quivered. He hadn't spoken to Fargo since the meeting—and looked like he didn't want to now. Spots of color stained his cheeks.

"Ten rifles! What do you want with ten rifles?"

"Do you have 'em or don't you?"

"Well, yes," McCutcheon said. "But I'll have to uncrate some. You'll have to come back. Who's gonna pay for these?"

Fargo straightened. "You'll think of something."

"A murderer under our own roof! Sweet Jesus witness our shame."

Caroline McCutcheon came into the store, clear eyes fixed on Fargo. Her lips were thinned to nothing and her nose was pinched and white. Fargo pulled off his hat.

"Blood on his hands and the stain of Satan on his soul." She said it casually, as if she were inquiring about his health or the weather. "You are certainly doomed to everlasting fire, young man. For he who harms God's creatures must stand at the altar of judgment and he will be surely damned."

"Caroline, please. . . ."

"Mr. McCutcheon, you grieve me. You treat with sinners and God is not in you."

"Go in the back, Caroline."

"While you entertain this beast under my roof? No. I will not."

Fargo looked from the woman to the anguished man. The storekeeper was twisting his hands in his apron; his wife stood still and tall, eyes fixed on Fargo.

"I'm leaving," he said. "Have the rifles ready. I'll send someone for 'em."

McCutcheon's wife was talking as he left, high and shrill. Something about taking the boy and leaving Gault when the pass opened. Everybody had troubles.

Fargo walked slowly up the boardwalk, savoring the sun. It was really warm today. He wore no coat; the flannel shirt was plenty. The snow was melting everywhere and the creek ran swollen. The street was a riot of thick mud, increased traffic churning it to gumbo.

"Hi, there, Marshal. Nice day. . . ."

He waved at the teamster who'd spoken. Shakey Burger stuck his head out of his shop. "Shave today, Mr. Fargo?"

"Who's next, Shakey?"

"You're always next, Marshal. Step right in."

"Busy, Shakey—thanks."

He passed on. There was a full shift on at the mine and the smelter was working. Gault was humming. A gawky boy and a young girl laughed aloud, picking their way through the mud.

"Mr. Fargo. Wait, please. . . ."

He turned. It was Nellie Dempster, hurrying up the walk as fast as her condition permitted. She carried a wooden box.

"Should you be running like that?"

She was out of breath and her color was high. She looked healthy and pretty.

"Oh, I'm fine. He's kickin' but he ain't due for a week or so. How you?"

"Fine, Nellie." They started slowly up the walk side by side. "Snow's going fast."

"Pass'll be open soon. Maybe the doctor can get up from Freemantle."

"What will you do, Nellie—after the baby comes? Go home? Back to your parents?"

She looked shocked. "Oh, no, I wouldn't do that. I'm healthy and strong and there ain't many women out here, you know. No, I'll find someone wants me, won't mind takin' the babies, too." She stopped him with a hand, looked up into his face. "I ain't disrespectin' Lloyd, Mr. Fargo. I loved him and made him a good wife. But he's gone and he ain't ever comin' back. I got to face that. I'm still here and so are my children. You understand?"

He nodded, looked away. "I understand, Nellie."

Abruptly she pushed the wooden box at him. "Here. This here's for you. Lloyd made it and I'd like you to have it."

He could think of nothing to say. He opened the box. Inside was a model in gold of a full-rigged sailing ship, all sails billowed. The workmanship was beautiful, each line in place, each plank a golden miracle of exactness. Fargo thought of the young miner, grubbing underground all day and sailing the seas of fancy at night as the little ship grew under his hands.

He shook his head. "No. Nellie, I can't take this."

"Listen," the girl said earnestly, "you take it. Lloyd he liked to work with his hands, you see. And he picked all them bits and pieces of gold out of the spoils himself. He liked you, Mr. Fargo."

She bit her lip. "I—I don't want it around—can't you see that? It'd keep him alive and he ain't and I got to go on livin'!"

She spun away and started back down the walk, head bowed. Fargo rubbed the box, absently. A man lives. A man dies. Nothing changes but the players.

He was slumped in his chair staring at the little ship on top of the desk when Bugle came in. The boy was quiet, subdued.

"Marshal, Miz Bragg she said tell you come right away."

"What's wrong, Bugle?" He got to his feet, got his hat.

The boy shook his head. He had his horn hung

'round his neck with a thong and he kept his eyes on it.

"Want to go with me?"

Bugle shook his head again, eyes down. Fargo got the Colt from the old holster, shoved it into his waistband.

"Something bitin' on you, Bugle?"

The boy's head came up slowly, "Did you—did you shoot McCall in the back?"

"Your Pa tell you that?"

"Yes. And he said I'm not to be around you. Not even say howdy. Did you, Marshal? Shoot him in the back?"

"Your Pa wouldn't lie to you, would he? Get on home."

Bugle stood shocked for a moment, then he broke for the open door. Fargo took a quick stride and caught the boy in the doorway.

"Bugle. Listen here a minute. And try to remember what I'm saying. A man is never all the way anything. You understand? Nobody is all good, or all bad—all hero or all anything." The boy's eyes stayed on his horn. "All of us, me, your Pa, you—we're all dabs of this and that and the other. All the things that go to make up a man. Some times, boy, bad things get done for real good reasons. I don't know how that balances out. Maybe nobody does."

Bugle said nothing, head down. Fargo touched a wild sprout of hair on the bent head. "You better go on home. . . ."

The boy turned and ran blindly down the muddy road. Fargo watched him out of sight. Then he pulled the door shut and started for Silesia's. The sun didn't feel as warm as it had before. Some of the sparkle had gone out of the day.

Brandy Culligan was an ugly man. There was a shallow depression in one temple and his nose was a twisted wreck. Broken veins splashed his cheeks above a scraggle of beard. But his eyes were fine, clear and blue, without guile. He was an itinerant miner, though mostly he worked for Silesia. Now, sitting at her table with an untouched cup of coffee, he was nervous and almost tongue-tied as Fargo waited for him to speak.

"Tell him, Brandy," Silesia urged. "Go on."

"Miss 'Lesia, them fellers'd have my neck if they know'd I even spoke to this—to the marshal. I got to live down there, y'see."

"Take your time," Fargo said easily. He walked to the fire. "Snow's melting fast, Silesia."

She nodded, eyes on Brandy. He looked up and she urged him silently.

"Marshal," Brandy said hesitantly, "Hobie and them fellers is fixin' to hit Gault. And right soon. They know the gold's hid down in the mine and they figure they got to kill you and take the town in order to get it. And that's what they aim to do before the pass opens."

"An attack in force. Can Spencer ride? How many men can he count on?"

"'Bout twenty, near as I can figure. Bad uns, that is. There's lots down there like me—ain't gonna do no fightin' one way or t'other. Hobie, he's all right—just a crease over his ear and a slug through his left hand." Brandy gulped coffee, made a face. "They think you're apt to get you some helpers. That new feller, he said that. Says you could train a dead jackass to fight, give you time enough."

Silesia saw Fargo grow still, all expression leaving his face. "New fella?"

"Yeah. The one says he come to kill you. Charlie something or other his name is. Him and Hobie's thick, I tell you. Some says he's a deserter but I wouldn't know about that. Miss 'Lesia, you got a small drop of something hereabouts? Just a—"

"Tell him," she said.

"Yes'm. This Charlie, he told Hobie that you was a deserter your ownself—from the cavalry." His eyes flicked to the breeches, the tell-tale yellow stripes.

"Hobie he bought me a bottle, told me to come up here and tell it around about you bein' a wanted man and on the run 'n all. I come to Miss 'Lesia and she said tell nobody nothin' and I ain't. That's all."

His blue eyes swung to Silesia. She nodded. Fargo frowned into the small fire. She got a jug of whiskey and gave it to the jittery miner.

"You get on back, Brandy. Tell Hobie you spread the word about the Marshal. Don't say nothin' about talkin' to him. Hear?"

"Just a minute, Mr. Culligan." Fargo turned. "This Charlie—he a stocky man, long side whiskers kind of reddish?"

"That's him. Got sand, too. Put a pistol on that crazy No-britches and backed him down. Can I go?"

"One more question. Can Hobie mount all his men?"

"Nope. Ain't near enough horses for all of 'em. 'Bout ten maybe twelve they got 'n that's all." He rose, cradling his jug, moved to the door. "You stop 'em, Marshal. I don't know how you kin, but—I hope you do."

He ducked through the door, fingers already working at the stopper of the jug.

Fargo blew out a long sigh. "That's it, then. They're coming, like I knew they would. And that town over there, that fat, happy, stupid town thinks everything is just dandy!"

Silesia got a cup of coffee and took it to him. He looked at her and the hard lines smoothed out a little.

"I like you in dresses. You know that, lady?"

Quick warmth leaped in her. She smiled. "Why you think I'm always wearin' one lately?"

He grew serious. "Silesia, this is bad. With Charlie Ward they'll be tough. Charlie's an experienced soldier, a good one. And he knows me, how I fight. You know how many volunteers I got from Gault? Six— two of 'em about sixteen years old. And none of 'em knows which end of a gun to point."

"I told you you'd get no help. And what you do

get'll only get in your way. They're miners—not soldiers."

His head came around. "What'd you say?"

"I just—just said whatever help you'd be likely to get over there'd be more hindrance than anything. . . ."

"Yes," he said, starting to pace. "You're right. And that might be it. That just might be it."

She watched him, striding the length of the cabin, back again. He moved like a jungle animal. His forehead was wrinkled in thought and he carried the forgotten coffee in one hand. She waited, content to look at him. He sat the cup on the table.

"I've got an idea, Silesia. It could work—if I'm very lucky and very fast and everyone does what they're told." He reached her in a stride, gripped her upper arms in those big hands. "You, I know I can count on. It's going to be a battle, you know that."

She nodded. "If they win, Gault will die. You can't let that happen, I guess."

He turned away, took off his hat and slapped it against his leg. "No, I can't. But I ought to. If I had the sense God gave a Christmas goose I'd hit that rimrock and not stop 'til my hat floated in the Pacific Ocean."

She moved closer to him, looked up, laying both palms flat on his hard chest. "You won't," she said, and her voice was husky, alive with sudden feeling. "Because you're Fargo and there's a fight to be fought. One you *have* got a stake in!"

"Yes . . . I have. I'm not sure that's good." Their glances locked and his eyes got smoky. "I'd better get going."

She slid her hands up to frame his face. "Stay here. I'll send you out to fight as a man should be sent."

His hands tightened on her waist. . . .

Chapter 11

"FARGO. . . ."

"Hmmm?"

"Want coffee?"

The glow from the fire was the only light and its flickering glow shadow-painted the cabin. Fargo moved stiffly on the familiar bed, lifted himself up on one elbow. Silesia stood near the fire wearing a long muslin wrapper. There was nothing at all masculine about the way it clung to her bountiful body. The mass of hair, like spun ebony, hung in heavy folds almost to her waist; it rippled with highlight when she moved. Watching her, remembering the feel and fury of her, his skin flushed warm.

"Silesia—come here."

She hung the coffee pot on the hook over the fire and moved to the bed with her lithe stride, bare feet whispering on the puncheon floor. As she sat on the edge of the bed, he propped himself against the back wall with a pillow.

"We've got to talk. I've never had to explain myself before so maybe I won't do it so good. I want to try, anyway."

"You don't owe me nothin', Fargo. I'm a grown woman."

"You told me not to get close, Silesia. It was good advice. We should have— Well, forget that. Brandy, your miner friend, what he said about me was true. I am a deserter. Six weeks ago, I ran from the guardhouse at Fort Denman to escape a firing squad."

It was very quiet. Far off creek-murmur, a snap from the fire. Silesia didn't move. She seemed not to breathe.

He leaned his head back against the rough logs of the wall, closed his eyes. "So—there it is. Time is running out for all of us. Especially for me and Charlie Ward. You see, he was guard sergeant the night I got away. He helped me."

"Then why is he—"

"Trying to kill me? He has to. You got to understand—Charlie was my best friend. Just about the only friend I ever had. But after he let me go that night, he shot me in the back as I ran."

Her breath hissed sharply.

"Yes. That's how it is. Me, and this hole in my back, that's Charlie's shame. He can't let me live and I don't blame him." He opened his eyes, looked at her. "I'm not going to stand and let him kill me. But I can see where he'd think he had to. There's more than that, too. But—" He sat straight, stretched his stiffened shoulders. "Could I have that coffee now?"

While she poured the coffee he got into his stained clothes, moved to the table. Silesia lit a smoky lamp and set it between them on the rough board. Then she sat across from him, watched him steadily through drifting steam from the coffee.

"Why?" she asked. "He was your friend, you said. He wouldn't just up and shoot you for nothin'."

"He had a reason. He was protecting himself." He sipped at the scalding coffee. "I was scheduled for trial the next day. He knew I'd do whatever I had to do to convince that court I wasn't guilty. And when I told my story in court—well, whether they believed me or not, Charlie would be in trouble. So he tried to shut me up with a bullet."

"What were you charged with?"

"Cowardice in the face of the enemy."

She straightened and her expression hardened. "I don't believe that."

His lips twisted. "Yeah. Well, that was the charge. You're right—it wasn't true. I did run. But not because of fear. Because I was the only one left and the position was about to be over-run."

"All the others had been killed?"

He looked down at the swirling liquid in his cup. The lines in his face deepened. "No. Here's how it was. The regiment was in Missouri—way up north—sort of resting up because we'd been in it from the first. Funny thing was, the war was already over when this thing happened at Wheeler's Hill. But we didn't know it. Word hadn't got to us yet. The old man sent out a regular ranging patrol. A half-troop under a brand new second john, fresh from the point. Pettigrew, his name was. I was regimental sergeant major and the old man sent me along to see the kid lieutenant didn't get into any trouble." He looked up, a tight smile twisting his lips. "I didn't do a very good job of it."

Silesia's hand came over the table, covered one of his. Her fine eyes were clear and very deep. "Go on. You've kept this inside too long."

He nodded, pushed the cup aside. "At that time, when the Confederacy was doomed and everybody knew it—well, the whole country went crazy. Deserters and thieves stealing and killing all over Missouri and Kansas. Men like Quantrill. And Eban Valentine, the Kansas Irregulars. Our patrol ran into one of those renegade bunches. About two hundred of 'em at Wheeler's Hill. We came up on them picking over the remains of one of our supply columns. All of the escort troopers had been killed and the rebs were looting and burning the wagons. You understand it was too late to save any of the soldiers. They were all dead. We were only a half-troop and even a pure-blind fool would know our job was to notify the regiment, maybe leave a couple dismounted scouts to keep contact. That's what I told Lieutenant Pettigrew. I thought he was going to shoot me. It was his first action and he wanted to fight. A kid lieutenant anxious to make his mark. Well, he made it—over the graves of fifteen men. Including his own."

Fargo pushed back the chair and paced slowly in

the warm cabin. The memory of that fight was still vivid; he couldn't sit still reliving it.

"You know what he did, that fool kid? Ordered a saber charge. A half-troop! Anyway, the surprise of it drove the rebs away from the wagons and we dug in there on top of the hill. By then we knew they were all around us and we were outnumbered by plenty. I told Pettigrew in plain language we better get the hell out of there—and fast. He wouldn't hear it. The renegades got organized and came back at us hard. We beat off the first rush but it cost a lot. Six dead and a couple more wounded. Pettigrew by then figured he was Custer and Meade all rolled into one. I made a formal request to retire in order and he went into some kind of a fit almost."

He stopped, unaware that he had, stared into a dark corner with blind eyes. He'd never forget the shrill voice of young Pettigrew, cursing, accusing. And the lead death whispering all around them in the Missouri dusk. *That crazy damn kid*. Fargo resumed his slow pacing.

"So the lieutenant he got out his map case and wrote out an order. On paper, signed and dated. We were to fight to the last man. It was stupid. There was nothing to win. No reward but a cold grave. But Pettigrew knew his chances to be a hero and win promotion were running out. At least in that war. So he wrote the battle order and that's what hung me, that little piece of paper."

Silesia stirred. "I don't understand."

"In war time, Silesia, a battle order is absolute. It must be obeyed. Besides—what happened at Wheeler's Hill was embarrassing to the army. They needed a goat and I was the highest ranking survivor."

"What happened to the lieutenant?"

"He ran," he said, and cut off her rising question with a gesture. "Didn't matter. He was killed before he got twenty feet. Before that happened we beat off another charge because Charlie Ward had found one of those new repeating guns in the supply train. Fires hundreds of rounds a minute, I don't know how many. It's a big heavy thing—something new. We got it together, Charlie and me, figured out how it worked and with it we stopped the second rush. I remember now Charlie was acting kind of funny. But I'd fought beside him for five years, a dozen battles. Him, I figured I could count on."

He walked to the table, slumped onto the chair. "In battle, nobody knows what they're gonna do. How they'll act until the time comes. Pettigrew had a small wound by then and was getting scared. He rescinded the battle order verbally. Nobody heard it except me. It was too late for us to get out then, anyway because they were coming back again and it seemed like there were thousands of 'em, screaming and firing. There were only six of us left. Me, Charlie, the lieutenant and three troopers. Against a couple hundred. That's when Charlie Ward broke and ran. The troopers saw him go, threw down their guns and went right behind him. Pettigrew tried to pull me away from the repeating gun but it was too late to get away without covering fire, so I stayed and cranked that thing. Oh, I wasn't being a hero. It was just the best thing to do. If we all up and ran, they'd grab us off or kill us easy with no return fire to slow 'em down. I stayed. And I stopped them again with the repeater. It's a hell of a gun. They weren't anxious to run that kind of a gauntlet."

"You should have got a medal! Not a firing squad."

Her cheeks were flushed and she was angry. For him. He shook his head. "Nobody saw it. The lieutenant and two of the troopers were killed before they got out of the clearing. Charlie and the other one got away in the dark. Later, the last trooper was found dead not far away. There was just Charlie and me left to tell about it. And I *did* run, you see. The rebs started up that hill again yelling like crazy and I knew there'd be no stopping them that time. So I ran. Right into two full troops coming to investigate the firing. They drove off the renegades. Then somebody found the paper on Pettigrew, and—well, that's it."

"But you could have told them how it was. Charlie could have helped you."

"Yeah. That's what I kept thinking. They pulled out the regiment right after that and sent us to Fort Denman. Me in chains all the way. I figured Charlie'd get around to telling it like it was and they'd let me go. I should have known better. He couldn't tell the truth without admitting he'd panicked first and run away like a raw recruit. He had my stripes by then and I guess he liked 'em."

Silesia got up slowly. Her brow was furrowed and her eyes hooded. She took the cups to the fireplace, poured fresh coffee and brought it back to the table. All without a word. Fargo watched her and wondered at the thickness in his throat from just looking at her.

"You've got to go," she said finally. "Either you or Charlie will die here if you stay. You know that. Without him, you can't get yourself straight with the army, can you?" He shook his head. "Then you gotta get out of here. Now—while there's a little time."

"Where will I go? Oregon country? California? Won't be long before they're states, too. Someday, somewhere there'd be a tap on my shoulder and I'd be all through. I don't like running, Silesia. Hell with it. Whatever's gonna happen, let it happen right here."

He took her hand, looked up at her. She worked up a tremulous smile for him, squeezed his hand.

"Listen!"

Neither moved. There was a spatter against the oiled paper on the window. Then a real gust and lightning cracked close by while thunder boomed overhead like monster surf.

"Rain. It's raining!"

Fargo sprang to the door, opened it. A rush of warm wind hit him as he stepped out into the night. Rain fell in scattered gusts carried by the wind. Lightning lanced again and for an instant the canyon was day-bright. Then the rain steadied and began pouring in a steady rataplan on the crusted snow. Silesia stood beside him, looking up, letting the warm rain hit her face.

"Chinook," she said. "If it keeps up all night the pass'll be open tomorrow."

Fargo tasted the water on his lips, smelled the freshness of the gentle wind. He laughed, wild and free, into the driving rain. He pulled her to him. The rain had plastered the thin muslin to her body; her face was slicked with moisture. He kissed her, hard—with promise and regret and a fierce kind of joy.

"They'll come now," he said. "Ready or not they've got to attack. Let's get busy."

He urged her back inside, looked around for his boots. In that moment the battle calm came to him. He recognized it, welcomed it. Always it had been that way. The prospect of danger made most men apprehensive, understandably afraid they might be hurt or killed. Not him. Never. Approaching danger had always chilled him, slowing the world down while his own reactions speeded. His mind would begin to race, considering probabilities, probing and rejecting until he had a certain knowledge of what was best to do in any threatening circumstance. He had never known fear and he felt none now. Something had been left out of his make-up and good or bad it had carried him through five years of war and it would carry him through this, too.

He stopped, one foot in a boot. Silesia stood quietly before the fire, eyes on him. Only this time it was different. There wasn't just himself to take care of—there was a whole town.

"Silesia—they'll hit us just before dawn." He stomped into the boot, stood. The tall clock by the door said ten o'clock. "We've got six hours—no more. You got loads for that rifle?"

"Yes. What do you want me to do?"

"Everybody on this side of the creek—you know

where they live? Can you get to all of 'em in the dark?"

She nodded. "Easy. Ain't but about fifteen all told."

"I want every one of them—and I mean all of them—right here in an hour. Take the rifle. If anybody balks, bring him anyway. Got it?"

She was already twisting her heavy hair into coils, winding it up out of the way. Fargo smiled appreciatively. Ten more like her and he'd fight a battalion. She grabbed up her rough clothes, went behind the dressing blanket hung in one corner.

"If I'm not back in an hour, wait for me. Don't let anyone leave. I'll get here. Those fools in town'll want to argue all night but I won't allow that. There's too much to do."

He got his hat, stuck the Colt into his waistband. He opened the door and Silesia heard it because she came out from behind the curtain with a rush.

"Wait." She wore the familiar trousers and the too-tight shirt, unbuttoned as yet. "You've decided what you're gonna do, haven't you?" He grinned at her disheveled appearance while she stamped a bare foot. "Don't be simperin' at me—tell me!"

He nodded, sobering. "All right. There's two pretty fair soldiers down there trying to figure how we'll defend this place. There's one thing they'll never anticipate and that's what I intend to do."

He paused, considered the whole thing again. All of the variables flashed through his mind as he reviewed the decision he'd made. It was right. He was sure of it.

"When the Spoilers ride into Gault tomorrow, Silesia, they won't find a living soul in town. Except me. . . ."

Chapter 12

WHEN THE RAIN started Charlie Ward was in the stable next to Savannah's, caring for his horses. It hadn't been a good day. He'd had a falling out with Hobie Spencer in the saloon and everybody heard it. Charlie wanted to hit the town right away and said so. He knew if they gave Fargo enough time he'd make Gault impregnable. Charlie didn't care about that, really. Whether or not the Spoilers got the gold was nothing to him. He just wanted a crack at Fargo. The sooner the better.

Hobie had been surly and half-drunk. He didn't drink much as a rule but he'd started early that morning and swilled steadily all day. When Charlie pressed for immediate attack, he had insisted they wait a day or two, hoping his wounded hand would get better. Anybody knew a day—or even a week—wasn't going to help a hand with a bullet hole through the palm. But Hobie was the Honcho and Charlie had finally stormed out of the place, after loud talk about a leader who didn't lead and didn't even seem very anxious to make any kind of preliminary preparations. He'd half expected a bullet in the back as he went out the door. Captain of the Zouaves! No wonder the rebels lost the war.

The stable was a sanctuary, even though it smelled like a fermenting swamp. For a long time Charlie had lived a life wherein a man took care of his animal before himself. The simple and automatic motions of cleaning and currying were familiar and soothing; he was glad to be alone. He had no liking for the men here. None of them were much good and Charlie had an honest man's distaste of parasites. He wasn't much of a drinker either, though he and Fargo had turned in a few memorable debauches here and there during the war.

Fargo. The name burned in his head. Fargo less than a mile away and here he was rubbing horses in a stinking stable by the light of a sputtering Bullseye lantern.

That's when he heard the rain. Immediately, he ran for the saloon, slipping and sliding through the melting snow. He burst inside, slamming the door back. There was a five-man poker game going and four men at the bar, Savannah behind it. No-britches crouched in his customary spot braiding strips of rawhide. No Hobie Spencer.

A thin, mean-looking man standing at the bar, said: "What the hell's the rush there, Sergeant?"

"Where's Hobie? I got to see him."

The thin man was J. T. Skeen, one of Hobie's gunmen. He had lank black hair, very long, and a drooping mustache to match. He grinned at the others, shook his head.

"Feature this here soldier. He rawhides the big man in front of everybody. Now, he wants to wake him up and him mean drunk." He turned back to Charlie and the smile dropped off. "You tired of livin', Ward?"

"It's important, Skeen. Goddam, man—can't you hear that rain?"

"What you want me to do—stop it?"

The men laughed and Charlie turned away and slammed a hand on the bar. "Damn fool! Savannah, you tell me where Hobie is."

"Just a minute!" Skeen's voice was loud. "Who you callin' a fool, soldier boy?"

Charlie turned from the bar, belly brick-tight and cold. His mutton-chops quivered.

"You listen, Skeen. Ain't no time for kiddy play right now. It's raining cover up hell out there. Warm rain—understand that? The pass'll be wide open by tomorrow night and that means we got no time left. But after this is over, we'll talk about who's a fool and who ain't."

He turned away and nobody said a word. The rain drummed on the frame building and thunder rolled, long and heavy. Charlie stopped in front of the Indian. No-britches had a skein of leather strips tied to a nail driven into the side of the piano. His brown fingers twisted and plaited. He looked up at Charlie without stopping his work.

"No-britches—that there's a chinook bringing the rain. I know you savvy that. Now you want to show me where Hobie is. . . ."

The bronze face didn't flicker. Little red flecks glowed in the Indian's eyes. He grunted, tied off his rawhide and stood.

"You come, White-eyes."

He strode out into the rain, knout dangling from his wrist. Charlie hastened after him, following the pale gleam of naked buttocks across the muddied yard to the building where Savannah's three girls were housed. No-britches pushed open the door, motioned for Charlie to go ahead of him. The Indian smelled worse than the stable.

The crib-house was a long building with a corridor running the length of it and doors leading off to one side. There was a shrill laugh, cut off with the sound of a slap. No-britches moved noiselessly to one of the doors. He jerked his head toward it and stood aside.

Charlie didn't hesitate. He pushed the door wide and stepped into the darkened room. He could make out figures in the rumpled bed against one wall. A bubbling snore came from one. Hobie Spencer and a very thin girl were entwined in sleep. Spencer was naked, his muscular body smooth and hairless like carved ivory. The girl wore a thin shift and nothing else.

"Hobie. Hobie, wake up!"

Charlie leaned over the man, shook him roughly. No response. Hobie was soused.

"No-britches, get some kind of a light in here."

He shook Hobie again, pulling him away from the lightly-clad woman beside him. She groaned and opened her eyes, blinking as the Indian brought a flaring oil lamp into the room.

"Say, what's— Who the hell'r you? What's—"

"Get up," Charlie said. The rust was heavy in his voice. He jerked the woman to her feet, shoved her toward the door. "Go wash your face. And bring some coffee back here right away. Understand?" The girl pushed at her messy hair, nodded vaguely. Her eyes were still sticky with sleep and love. "Go on. If you're not back in ten minutes I'll send the Indian after you. Git!"

She got. No-britches made small sounds in his throat, his face impassive as ever. He was laughing. Charlie got hold of one of Hobie's arms, pulled him upright and twisted the inert body so that the side wall propped him up. He was still out cold, chin on chest.

"Hobie, come out of it, man. It's Ward. You got to wake up!"

The big head stirred, lifted a bit, fell again. Charlie slapped him, one hand then the other. Hard, stinging slaps. Hobie's head jerked up, the marble-like body clenching. His eyes opened but they were glazed.

"What the hell?" He recognized Charlie. "You! It comes to me, Fren Sharlie—I think I'll—"

Charlie got the water pitcher from the washstand and up-ended it over Hobie's head. The outlaw sucked an outraged breath as the cold water poured over him. He surged up from the bed. Charlie pushed him back with one hand, drew his Colt with the other.

"Now, hold it, Hobie. I said, hold it!"

The man's eyes were murderous and there was no sign now of drink glaze in them. The wide face was a mask of fury.

"Listen to me. I had to wake you, man. It's raining. You hear me? It's raining—right now!"

Comprehension came into Hobie's look. His body

relaxed, slumping back against the wall. He listened for a moment, registering the sound of pelting raindrops on the building. Lightning flashed outside and lit the tiny room through the single window. Hobie sighed mightily, rubbed his good hand over his face. He sat up on the side of the bed.

"A couple of slaps, if you would be so kind, Sergeant. And put the pistol away. Come, come, man—you were not so squeamish a few moments ago. Slap me."

Charlie did, not holding back. The huge head barely moved on the pillar of neck muscle. Hobie held up a hand.

"Sufficient. Now, then. . . ." He hooked a chair with a foot and pulled it to him, began donning the clothing piled upon it. "So, Sergeant—you were right it appears. We must move right away. No-britches!" The Indian glided close. "Get everybody up. You know who they are. Armed and ready in thirty minutes at Savannah's. All of them, you understand—sick, sober, sorry or crippled, I want everyone there ready to ride at daylight. Move."

The Indian vanished noiselessly. Charlie walked to the window and stared out at the driving rain. Already the mass of snow was receding. Above the sound of the storm came the growing roar of the swollen creek.

"You said daylight, Hobie?"

"You object, sir?" Spencer's voice was again modulated, cultured, a touch sardonic. "From your lofty vista as a former non-commissioned officer—who has, incidentally, never seen our objective—do you perceive something which eludes my more pedestrian vision? Well?"

Charlie swung around, pointed a finger at the man on the bed. "You talk pretty, Spencer. And you might have been a captain like you say. But I'll tell you something—you make this a textbook attack, a manual exercise, and we'll all be deader'n a week ago Friday."

Hobie pulled on a boot, looked at Charlie thoughtfully. "You mean, I presume, our mutual and respected enemy, Fargo. You fear his influence upon those mice up there."

"That's what I mean."

There was a knock on the doorframe. The thin girl, swathed to the throat in a shapeless robe, entered hesitantly. She carried a tray with a coffee pot and two cups which she placed on the washstand.

Hobie said, "Get out. Don't let anybody back here except the Indian."

The girl scurried out. Charlie poured a cup of the steaming brew, handed it to Spencer.

"Ah. Very good. You know, Ward—in some ways you are an exemplary man. But I'm a bit suspect, you see, of your judgment in this. You pursue vengeance. A poor spur, to turn a phrase." He leaned back, gulped at the hot liquid avidly. "Liquor, friend Charlie—the curse of the thinking man. Now. Summarize for me, please."

It was a command. Charlie instinctively stiffened. Then he nodded in assent. "All right, Hobie. First—it's raining up there in Gault, too, you know. Fargo knows as well as we do the attack has to be tomorrow. He'll figure dawn. He'll be ready. You hit entrenched positions in daylight, he'll chop us up like Army hash."

Hobie stood, stretched. He moved to the small mirror over the washstand, began currying his mustache.

"What it hangs on," Charlie went on, "is your bunch gettin' them hostages. Wait'll daylight and Fargo'll have the women and kids so wrapped in protection you won't get near 'em."

The wide man turned from the mirror. He pulled a watch from his vest, opened the cover. "Almost eleven."

Charlie said nothing. Hobie got into his gunbelt, clumsy with his injured hand. He examined it near the light, flexed the fingers, unable to hide a pain spasm as he did so.

"Would you believe, friend Charlie, that at one time

Hobart Remington Spencer aspired to be a great virtuoso? A concert performer? Very true. Yes. Imagine this lumpy body, these—" He held up his huge hands—"on a stage before an audience of quality. An ape in a dress suit, they said." There was a smile on the thick lips but no mirth was in it. "Yes. My idiot brother had the face, the figure. And I had nothing but the soaring ability, the burning desire. They laughed before I played a note. The fools laughed!"

He strode abruptly to the window, stared out through the streaming pane.

"All right, Sergeant." The voice was soft again, under control. "I agree with your estimate. What do you recommend?"

"The same plan, Hobie. Just this—send a man up both sides of the canyon along the rimrock. On foot. I'd say No-britches for one. And whoever else you got can move good. They should leave right now."

Hobie nodded. "And the rest of us go when?"

"Just as soon as we can get 'em moving."

"That's what we'll do." Spencer started for the door, Charlie right behind him.

The pelting rain hit them outside and Hobie stood for a moment smelling the air and letting the raindrops bathe his face. Charlie jittered impatiently beside him.

"Damn it, Hobie—time is what we can't waste. Let's get on with it."

The outlaw turned his wide-eyed gaze on him.

"Ward, I pray that you survive this little adventure. I truly do. Then the pleasure of killing you will be mine. . . ."

Chapter 13

THE RIFLES WERE new and shining. McCutcheon had begun uncrating them with the first spatter of rain on his shutters and now he and Bugle were cleaning the last of the preservative from the Henrys, testing the action and loading them. The store was dark save for one bracket lamp near the counter illuminating the line of weapons laid neatly across the board.

Twelve repeating rifles. Death for how many people in their full magazines? McCutcheon shook the thought away, applied himself to the gun in his hands. His son industriously rubbed at the stock of another, with an oiled rag. The rain had settled to a steady patter. Big drops that hit the shutters hard.

Andy sighed and looked at his watch. Eleven-ten. Over an hour since the rain started and still Fargo hadn't come for the guns. He would, McCutcheon knew. Because with the rain and the chinook melting the snow like magic, the Spoilers would have to make their play for the gold immediately.

"Pa. . . . You think they'll come shootin'—Hobie and them?"

"Well, son, they'll come. I'm sure of that. Keep that cloth well soaked. With this rain the more oil on these things the better."

The boy nodded. He worked soberly and carefully, doing a good job. McCutcheon smiled, watching him. Then he remembered what the morning might bring and the anxiety came back, cold and prickling.

"We gonna fight 'em, Pa?"

"We'll have to, I guess. I don't know how or where but— Well, we'll leave that up to Marshal Fargo."

The boy's eyes lifted, held steady on his father's face. McCutcheon became very busy.

"You see, boy, fightin' is a special job. A man has to know how if he's gonna do it nearways good. Fargo, he knows how so we'll listen to what he says. He's—I mean, we're lucky he's here."

His face burned and he bent over the rifle.

"That ain't what you said before."

"I know." He looked up; Bugle was still looking at him. "I said a lot of things I'm ashamed of, Andrew. Your Ma—yippin' at me about going somewhere else, takin' you because of the killing and all. Near had me looney. Bugle, I want this here town to grow, get prosperous and solid. I want you to be able to say someday your father helped build it. You see?"

"Yessir. Only you said Fargo was a bad man. I wasn't to go near him."

McCutcheon drew a deep breath through the sudden stricture in his chest. He nodded. "Yes, I did. I was jealous, son. The way you looked at him, talked about him. Man wants his boy to have only one hero, I guess. That's wrong. I know that now and I'm sorry I was weak. I told you Fargo shot Sudden Jack McCall in the back and that's true, he did. What I didn't say was McCall had shot twice at the marshal and was turnin' to put a bullet in me when Fargo fired."

"Then it wasn't his fault. He saved your life. . . ."

Andy nodded, relieved now that he'd unburdened himself. The boy's brow was twisted as he sorted the new feelings. He grinned, finally, started to speak. Caroline's voice cut sharply through the gloom.

"Andrew. Come away from that devil's work. Right now." She walked into the circle of light. "Come, son. I want you to pack your things."

Bugle did not move. McCutcheon stood slowly, a rifle forgotten in his hands.

"Pack his things? What are you sayin', woman?"

"The pass will open with this weather, husband. As you well know. I intend to leave this cruel place, forsaken by God and dripping with the blood of His children."

Her eyes were alight with fervor. Andy stared at her, incredulous. He had never believed she would really do it. Not after ten years and all they'd been through.

"Caroline, listen to me." He placed the rifle with the others, turned back to the stiff woman who was his wife. "You're back there packin' to leave, is that it?"

"It is. And past time. I never should have stayed this long."

Bugle slid around the counter and out of sight.

"Well you'll have to stay a little longer, Caroline. What's wrong with you? Don't you know what's goin' on around you? Half a mile down the canyon there's a whole army of thieves and killers fixin' to take this town apart. And you're gonna ride right through 'em with a Hallelujah and Praise the Lord!"

"Don't blaspheme! Your soul is black enough."

"And you're blind! Hobie and his men are coming after that gold. They know it's here and they're gonna come after it!"

"Then give it to them! Let them take the gold, let them take the town before you shed one drop of Christian blood in its protection."

McCutcheon shook his head, bewildered. "I can't fight your scriptures. I know this town will dry up and blow away if we lose that gold. Maybe the Book says turn the other cheek and maybe that was right for them old-timey people. I ain't turnin' my cheek. This town has a life, too. The people make it live and in return it gives them sanctuary and food and good, honest work." He swept an arm indicating the store, the town, the canyon. "This here's ten years of my life and I ain't leavin'."

"What town?" The scorn in her voice burned. "This miserable, Godless mess? Let it die! Let it shrivel to a crisp like Sodom! Let it—"

"Shut your mouth!"

It was a roar. Caroline stood open-mouthed with shock. A thunderous pounding shook the front door. Andy turned slowly from his wife, still choked with anger. He went to the door and lifted the heavy bar. Fargo pushed it open, stood aside as half the town trooped into the store shaking the wet from clothes and hats.

Foster Prudhomme said, "Andy, time's getting short. Fargo's got a plan to beat the Spoilers and we got to talk about it."

About thirty men had pushed in from the rain, Fargo last. He slapped his sopping hat against his leg, went right for the line of rifles on the counter.

"Mr. McCutcheon." It was Caroline, spots of red in her cheeks and chin thrusting like a blade. "I will not be a party to sin and violence. Get these people out of here."

Andy reached his wife in one swift stride, gripped her arm tightly. "You listen, woman. Get on in the back until I tell you to move. Understand? If I hear one more word I swear 'fore that God you love so well I'll beat you blue!"

The woman backed up two steps, hand at her cheek. Then she turned and ran to the door and out of sight.

"All right, man," Foster Prudhomme said. "Let's get down to it. We only got a couple of hours. Now this is what Marshal Fargo thinks we should do. . . ."

Silesia's clock struck softly, twice for the half-hour. Thirty minutes before midnight. The cabin was hot and stuffy and crammed with people. Eleven men and three women, not counting her. She sat on the bed, Sam's rifle across her knees and considered the miners and their wives filling the chairs, lounging on the floor. Talk had stopped. They were getting restless. She wished Fargo would come.

"Silesia," Burt Stapleton said. "How long we gotta wait for that fella? A hour, you said."

"He'll be here, Burt. And so will all of you."

"Well, now—I don't know about that. I got other things to do. This rain tearin' up my sluice 'n all."

"How about Hobie Spencer and the rest comin' to tear up Gault? You gonna do something about that, are you, Burt?"

The man's truculence faded; he growled and slumped further down against the wall.

Silesia said, "We'll wait. All of us. Like Fargo said to."

The rain drummed steadily.

Savannah's place was in uproar. Twenty-one men cursing nervously, preparing guns and honing knives. It was a scene out of madness with the rain pouring down, the roar of the creek and an occasional flash of lightning. Charlie paced nervously, walking to the door to check the horses, then back inside to listen as Hobie briefed his men. The squat leader stood at the table with J.T. Skeen, the Indian No-britches, and a wild-looking buckskin-clad man with a rifle taller than himself.

"Hobie, what time is it?"

Spencer looked at him without expression. "Not yet midnight, Sergeant. Simmer down. We'll be gone in an hour. Long before they expect us up there." He turned back to Skeen. "We have twelve horses, none of them in the best of shape. You get all but two, J.T. Pick your nine men and get the horses ready. And remember—when you strike, strike hard and fast. Make all the noise you can so the rest of us can get across the creek further up without undue notice."

"I got it. How we gonna know when y'all got the hostages?"

"Watch the jail. You know where that is. It's high on the slope and you will be quite able to see it at all times. When you see a lantern hanging in front, it will mean we have the hostages and you then disengage and bring all of your men to the jail. Understand?"

"Yeah, yeah. How come you don't send this here hotshot soldier with us?"

Hobie's massive hand flicked out, slammed against Skeen's cheek, knocking the man to his knees. He grabbed the table, pulled himself erect.

"Any more questions, Mr. Skeen?" The man shook his head, face pale except for a livid spot on one cheek. "Excellent. Sergeant Ward, show J.T. which of the horses he is not to take."

"No need. Ours are outside saddled and ready. He takes all the others."

"Very efficient, friend Charlie. I expected no less. Back here, Skeen, when you've picked your men and prepared your mounts." He turned away from the thin man, looked toward the bar where Savannah and one of her girls were cutting white sheeting into strips. "Hurry that up, Savannah. Two for each man and bring me four right now, please."

The woman hurried over with a handful of the cloth strips. Charlie and Hobie tied a white strip to the upper arms of the two scouts.

"Get a man shot, that will," the buckskin man muttered.

"More likely keep him from getting shot by his own people, Turkey. You keep them on." Hobie stepped back and indicated the two men with a wave. "There you are, Sergeant. Your scouts. Brief them if you please, sir, and send them along."

He turned away in dismissal. Charlie examined the two. They looked capable enough, all right. No-britches had expanded his armament. He carried a pair of light throwing axes stuffed through his beaded belt. A wide band of black paint crossed his nose from cheek to cheek; yellow and red lines ran here and there on his face and forehead. He was stripped to the waist and a strange, bluntly-drawn bird with outstretched wings decorated the naked chest. The other, Turkey Tom, was a mountain man. Fringed buckskins, moccasins and a long rifle. He wore no hat, his graying hair hanging in two braids. He smelled as bad as the Indian.

Charlie sighed. "All right. Let's get on outside and I'll show you where I want you to go."

Foster Prudhomme shouted vainly for quiet. The long store, lit now by everything available, was a muttering mass of miners and business men—all angry. Fargo wrapped a new slicker around another of the rifles, fastened it. He was going to have to stop this bickering soon. Time was getting by.

"Listen," Shakey Burger said. "It just don't make no sense. One man against twenty'r more. No sense."

The others agreed, loudly. Prudhomme, his prominent teeth bared, pounded a rifle butt on the floor until it got quiet.

"Will you listen? It does make sense. It's the only way. Fargo, tell them like you told me."

Fargo put the swathed rifle beside six similar bundles on the counter. He turned to Bugle McCutcheon crouched in the shadow with his horn. "Bugle, take that bowl of gun-oil and put about half a cup of soot in it from the fireplace. Mix it up then bring it back to me. All right?"

The boy rose swiftly, hung his bugle around his neck and ran toward the back cradling the bowl of oil.

"Now," Fargo said, "let's get down to it. If I was Hobie and half-way smart, this is what I'd do. What I want is the gold. Right? The easier I can get it the better I like it. I'd suspect that Fargo would fortify a few of these buildings down-canyon and I wouldn't want to come up that narrow pass into rifle fire from men behind cover."

"Well, why don't we do that?" a young, red-faced miner asked. "There's more of us."

"I'll tell you why. Because you wouldn't get much to shoot at and none of you can shoot, anyway. I'm Hobie, right? I send a loud and careful attack at the strong point. Then I send another bunch up the other side of the creek, cross 'em further up and hit the houses and shacks up near the mine. I'd get all the women and children I could gather. Men, too. Anybody I came across—but for sure the women and kids. Then I'd send word to the brave defenders of Gault to lay down their arms and deliver up the gold or their families will die. I'd figure you'd give up the gold right quick that way." He looked around. There was no sound except the incessant rain. "That's what I'd figure —if I was Hobie Spencer. Would I be right. . . ?"

The men shifted nervously. One said, "Would they do that? They get the women and young'uns, we're done."

"All right," the red-faced miner said. "Put the families in the mine, most of the men, maybe. But some of us can fight and by God I'm going to!"

Several others murmured agreement. Fargo picked up one of the unwrapped rifles from the counter. He jacked the shells out of the magazine.

"What's your name?"

The miner stepped forward. "Alva Hawkins—and what makes you think we won't fight for what's ours?"

Fargo threw the Henry at the man. He caught it clumsily, held it like a shovel. Fargo gave him some shells.

"Load it."

Hawkins held the rifle awkwardly, tried to find where the shells went into it. After a moment, he shook his head sheepishly.

"All right," Fargo said gently. "You see what I mean? In the war we found out raw recruits were worse than none at all. Because we had to worry about them and about ourselves, too. That's why I want all of you people out of the way." Bugle came back with the bowl of oil, now a thick, sooty mess. "Thank you, son. Put it on the counter."

"What's that for?" Prudhomme asked.

Fargo waved the question aside. "Time's getting on. What I want you men to do is get your families and take them to the mine. Prudhomme will show you where. One man with a rifle can hold a mine tunnel against a regiment. You'll need water, a little food—not much. Blankets, lamps—get all those things and get moving. We'll put a man up on the rimrock behind the town where he can see past the bend. He'll let us know when he sees the Spoilers. Mr. Kunz—" He nodded toward the owner of the town livery stable— "will hammer on that wagon tire in his yard. That means everybody get to the mine, fast. Clear?"

"It's clear to me," Andy McCutcheon said. "I'll go along with Fargo."

Someone said, "They can starve us out."

"No they can't." Fargo dipped his fingers in the soot and oil, began spreading it over his hands and wrists. "The pass'll be open tomorrow. People will be coming in. Besides—I won't be in the mine. And I intend to make it uncomfortable for them to stay around very long."

He took more blacking and applied it to his face and neck. Wherever skin showed he smeared the black stuff. With the hat on, the dark mackinaw buttoned tight, he'd be all but invisible in the dark.

"Hawkins—you want to help?" The man nodded eagerly. "All right—take these." He handed him two of the slicker-wrapped rifles. "Put one on the roof of the mine office and one on top of the Dempster house. Got that? And take one of these for yourself to defend the tunnel. Get going."

The man nodded, took the three weapons and went out into the rain. Prudhomme looked at his watch.

"Forty past twelve, Marshal."

Fargo nodded. He gave three more slicker-wrapped rifles to men as they left with instructions as to where they should be planted. He took the two remaining bundles under his own arm.

"Let's get moving. There's no guarantee Hobie will wait till dawn." He looked around for Bugle but couldn't see him anywhere. "Well, Foster. If we pull this off I guess we'll all be surprised."

The little mine manager looked at him, shook his head wordlessly and hurried out into the swirling night.

Andy McCutcheon said, "Fargo. I want to tell you that—"

Fargo held up one blackened hand. "No time for tears, McCutcheon. I'll say this—a man has a lot better chance to run a town after he's learned to run his own house. Better get busy."

He stepped out into the slanting rain, headed for Silesia's. The ground was an impossible quagmire—water rushing down the slope toward the creek, mud ankle deep where the snow had gone entirely. No moon, no stars. Black sky and sticky rain.

Lousy weather to die in. . . .

Chapter 14

THE RAIN WOULD make it tough. Footing was bad. Where the snow had not melted completely away it was hard-crusted and icy. Everything else was mud. And visibility was limited. Fargo, slithering down the bank of the creek, could see nothing but dark sheets of wind-blown rain. He plunged into the current. The water came almost up to his waist and he had to struggle to keep his feet. It wasn't exactly an ideal battleground. But it would have to do.

He made his way up the slope to Silesia's cabin with difficulty. There was light coming through the oiled paper of the window, through the cracks in the door. No sound, though. He lifted the latch and stepped inside.

Shocked silence and Silesia pointing a rifle right at

his brisket. Then he remembered the blacking on his face; they didn't recognize him.

"Hold it. It's me." He pushed the door closed behind him. "Put that thing down, Silesia."

There was a babble of excited voices and he ignored it, leaning the two streaming bundles containing the rifles against the wall near the door.

Silesia said, "You're late. But I kept them here. This is everybody from this side."

He nodded. "All right, people—listen. I've just had all the bickering and discussion I need for one night. So I'll just tell you what I want you to do."

Quickly he outlined the plan for them. There were a few murmurs of dissent but he talked right over them. He was a little irritated and it showed in his manner. It was hot in the cabin and he steamed inside the soaked mackinaw. His boots squelched. He was wet clear through and likely to remain that way for some time.

"That's it. When you hear the alarm, everybody get up here to Silesia's and into her mine. Any of you that have guns, bring 'em along. Blankets, water—you know what you need. Don't come out until you're absolutely sure it's safe. That may be soon and it may be a day or two. Depends on how the fight goes."

"I don't like it," Burt Stapleton said. "I'd as soon fort up in my soddy."

"Go ahead," Fargo said. "Don't look for any help. Everybody else will be underground."

"Except you."

"That's right," Silesia said. "Except him. So shut up Burt and go do like the man says. Leave the women here and go get what we need. Go on."

Slowly, the miners drifted out leaving only the three women, Fargo and Silesia. She brought him a stiff drink of whiskey and he gulped it down gratefully.

"That's good. Gonna be a long night."

"Fifteen after one. What time you reckon they'll come?"

He shrugged. "No telling for sure. I'd say just before

dawn. I want to leave one of these rifles around somewhere outside. Where I can get to it in a hurry if I need it."

He picked up one of the bundles and stepped outside. She was right beside him.

"You'll get wet, honey."

"I'll live." She gripped his arm. "Why don't you put that in the stable? Best place I can think of."

She took the rifle from him and led the way to the stable. The ponies shifted restlessly as they entered. Silesia shushed them. She put the rifle in the far corner and rejoined him near the entrance. Water dripped through the roof. Fargo started to take her in his arms, remembered the blacking all over his hands.

Silesia slid her arms around his waist, pulled herself against him, looking up. "You could still get out, Fargo. It's not too late."

His eyes moved slowly over her face, feature by feature, as if to burn a picture of her into his brain.

"Yes it is, Silesia. It was too late the minute you pulled me out of that snowdrift."

She kissed him—oil, soot and all. In the middle of the kiss, he stiffened, pushed her away abruptly.

"What's wrong?"

"It may be too late for all of us. I forgot to put a lookout up on the rimrock."

The yard of Savannah's place was sodden confusion. Horses and men and unending rain. Charlie kneed his horse away from the seven men standing at the creek bank. Everybody was soaked and miserable and they hadn't started yet. He rode up beside Hobie, sitting his animal in front of the porch on which stood J.T. Skeen. Hobie wore a dragoon coat of white leather, already glistening with wet. He'd make a fine target.

"Give us five minutes," Hobie was saying. "Then mount up and ride straight up the road to Gault. Don't stop and don't wait for any signals. When you get there, start shooting. By then we'll be in position across the creek. We won't cross into the upper town until we hear your firing, so don't wait."

Skeen said, "Five minutes, we ride. We'll be there, you get the women." He grinned wickedly showing stained and broken teeth. "Save one of 'em for me."

Hobie stood in the stirrups. "Remember, men—whoever gets that marshal—that Fargo—gets a double share of the gold. Let's tear us up a town!"

The men cheered. Hobie swung his horse toward the creek.

"I'll go first, Sergeant. Follow behind and keep these fools together."

He rode straight into the rushing water and the seven men on foot plunged in right behind him. Charlie wiped the rain from his face, halted his mount at the creek bank waiting for the walking men to get across. It was a good plan. Nine of them up the blind side of the creek. Skeen's ten horsemen to make the initial assault right up the road. No-britches and Turkey Tom above the town on both sides of the canyon. They'd have Gault in a box.

A box even Fargo wouldn't be able to find a way out of. Charlie urged his horse into the black-running creek.

Andy McCutcheon hurried up the slight incline of the mine's main tunnel. Sputtering lamps were spaced here and there attached to the shoring. Still it was gloomy and Andy stumbled on the unfamiliar ground. Farther back in the mine, where he'd just left Caroline, the underground labyrinth was a madhouse. Women keening and babies bawling, the smell of raw fear and damp clothing filling the crowded chamber. And only a few of the town's inhabitants had arrived yet. How it would be when they'd all crowded into the rock-walled sanctuary he hated to think.

Caroline had curiously given him no trouble at all, gathering blankets and coats, following him docilely. When he left her just now she had begun quieting the more excitable women, started organizing work for everybody. Not a word of Scripture. Nothing about leaving Gault.

He felt a tremor underfoot and a high-sided, iron ore car rumbled out of the gloom ahead of him. Three rain-soaked miners controlled it against the pitch of the tunnel. Foster Prudhomme hovered behind, barking comments and commands. The mayor was dripping like the others, his hard hat pulled down until it dented the tops of his ears. He wore a large slicker which scraped the ground as he walked.

"Stand aside, Andy. Got to get this car down there."

McCutcheon got against the wall, next to a shoring timber as the miners maneuvered the heavy car past him. He grabbed Prudhomme's arm as he would have gone on by.

"Foster, wait. I've got to talk to you."

Prudhomme called to the miners, "Wait a minute. Now, what Andy Mac? The whole town's gone crazy. Everybody running and nobody knows where Fargo is. If we get out of this I swear I'll never look at another mine."

"Fargo's across the creek. Organizin' them others. We got time, Foster—dawn's four or five hours away. The folks'll get below ground in time. But I'm worried about Bugle. I can't find him. You seen him anywhere?"

"Your boy?" Prudhomme clenched his lips over his buckteeth. "You can't find him? Sure he ain't down there with the others?"

"I'm sure. I just come from there. I'm gonna go look for him."

"Wait, I'll go with you." He addressed the waiting miners. "Get that car down to stope fourteen. Where the fall makes that turn. Turn it crossways facing up this way and pack one side with anything you can get. Leave one side open between the car and wall so's the people still coming in can get by. You got that, Murray?"

A gray-haired miner nodded. "Yeah, Foster. Who we goin' to put behind it with the rifles? I can't shoot even a little bit."

"We'll figure that out later. There's time. Come on, Andy." He started up the tunnel, McCutcheon hurrying with him. "Can't shoot! As if a man has to be a marksman to fire up a tunnel. Why Bugle could hold this shaft against the Mexican army, firing from behind a barricade."

They reached the entrance and stepped out into the rain. It hadn't abated any; the warm wind still blew the drops in slanting sheets. A group of townspeople materialized out of the murk.

"Where do we go, Foster? My kids is soaked."

It was Shakey Burger and his family.

"Straight down the fall, Shakey. Murray'll show you. Anybody seen McCutcheon's boy?"

Head shakes. Anxiety stabbed Andy and he started down the slippery slope toward town, almost running. Damn kid. When he found him he'd paddle him good, scaring everybody like this. His feet slipped in the mud and he fell, tangled in the slicker. A strong hand gripped his arm and lifted him effortlessly back to his feet. It was Fargo, the black mess on his face streaking with rain.

Foster Prudhomme slogged up. "You trying to kill yourself, Andy? That won't help Bugle."

"I got to find him," Andy muttered. His face was mud-covered and cold. "Fargo, you seen Bugle? Is he over at Silesia's? I can't find him. I can't find him!"

"Take it easy," the big man said. "He's around somewhere. Don't panic, Andy—you're doing just fine. Both of you listen. We have to get a man up on that rimrock right away. If they rode in on us now without any warning it wouldn't even be a contest. Where's that fella, Hawkins? The one said he wanted to fight?"

"Down at McCutcheon's," Prudhomme said. "I sent him for guns and some shells."

Fargo turned and took off down the hill, sure-footed

even in the slop. The little mayor and Andy followed more slowly. Fargo swerved into the livery yard. Kunz was huddled in the stable doorway.

"Stand by, Kunz," Fargo said. "There's a lot of people depending on that alarm."

The fat man nodded, brandished a hammer. "I be here, Marshal. Big noise I make, you tell me when."

Andy paused to ask the man about Bugle. Kunz hadn't seen him. Nobody had. He ran after Fargo and Prudhomme, the boardwalk giving him better footing.

There was an ore wagon with a four-hitch of mules in front of the store and a group of sodden men on the wide boardwalk. Fargo had the miner, Hawkins, by one arm, talking quickly and pointing up toward the vantage he wanted the man to watch from.

Lightning stuttered across the inky sky. For a long moment the canyon was day-bright. Even after the light had died, Andy could see the scene outlined on his eyeballs in reverse contrast.

Fargo called to him: "McCutcheon. Give Hawkins your slicker. He'll need it up there. Hurry!" He turned to Prudhomme as Andy struggled out of the muddied slicker. "Foster—send that wagon on up to the mine. One of you others make sure Nellie Dempster and her kids get up there all right. And keep an eye out for McCutcheon's boy. Move!"

A new sound cut through the night—the staccato notes of a cavalry bugle, strident and imperative. It came from down-canyon and high up the town-side slope.

"It's Bugle!"

Andy started off the boardwalk, heading for the rimrock and his son. Fargo swept him off his feet, both huge arms around him. He struggled, kicking with both feet. He felt himself slammed against the store; a hard palm cracked his cheek. He stood, stunned.

Fargo held him with one hand on his chest. "Be still! They're coming—don't you understand that? Bugle climbed the rimrock with his horn and that's what he's telling us. The Spoilers are coming right now!"

Everyone stood as if frozen. Fargo turned his head toward them, keeping Andy pinned to the store.

"Listen! Get everybody into the mine right now. Prudhomme—get them moving, man. Hawkins, go with them. We had a lookout all the time." He released the pressure on Andy's chest, spoke softly for him alone. "All right, Andy Mac. Let's go get your son."

He followed the big man blindly, senses spinning with shock and fear and the reverberating clangor of Kunz's alarm. The bugle had stopped. Andy pushed down his anxiety and concentrated on keeping up with Fargo. He moved fast, bent-kneed and crouching, angling up the hill and down-canyon. McCutcheon's breath roared and his muscles protested—but he kept up somehow. Fargo called the boy every fifty feet or so.

Suddenly, there he was, mud-covered and soaking wet, sliding down the rain-rutted mountainside. Andy grabbed the boy, unable to speak. He held him tight and closed his eyes.

"I'm all right, Pa. I saw them. They're comin' up the road and they ain't far off."

Fargo gently pulled him from the boy. "How many, Bugle, could you see?"

"I saw 'em good, Marshal—in the lightning. Maybe a dozen and all horseback. They was almost to the bend."

"No time, then. Let's go."

He picked Bugle up and started back down toward the town. Andy followed, facing into the slanting rain. It took them what seemed an eternity to get down the treacherous slope to the back of the store. Fargo put the boy on his feet, led the way between the store and the next building.

"Get on the boardwalk," he said. "It's faster. Don't stop running 'til you—"

He stopped abruptly, held them back with an outstretched arm. They had reached the steps leading up to the continuation of the boardwalk and Fargo crouched behind the wooden stairway. He stared into the rain-streaked dark. Lightning lit the canyon briefly and Andy saw what the marshal must have somehow sensed—a group of men moving up the other side of the creek. Between them and the mine. They pushed back against the side of the building out of sight.

"Too late," Fargo breathed. "We're cut off. Andy, take Bugle into the store. The back way. Get out of sight and don't make a sound. Come on!"

He led them to the rear door, peered around the corner of the structure, watching the road down-canyon. Andy pushed the boy inside.

"Bugle said a dozen, Fargo. At least ten in that bunch we saw. Long odds against one man. Let me help."

Fargo turned from his scrutiny of the road.

"Do like I told you. Stay quiet, stay out of sight. I'll see about shortening those odds right now. . . ."

Chapter 15

THEY CAME OUT of the dark, shadow figures out of deeper shadow, horseman shapes made indistinct and shimmering by the falling rain. Ten men on shaggy horses stumbling in fetlock-deep mud. They stopped fifty yards below McCutcheon's store and huddled together blending into one dark blotch. Fargo narrowed his eyes to improve the focus. The horsemen were too far away; he couldn't identify any of them at this distance.

He slid the barrel of his Henry out between the

plank steps of the boardwalk. He was under the porch of Burger's barber shop and not happy about it. He had intended making his initial attack from the roof of the store—a much better vantage. Now, he couldn't afford to draw fire to that building with McCutcheon and Bugle inside.

A rebel yell split the darkness. The Spoilers came on, kicking their mounts into ragged motion up the muddy street. It was a straggly, uneven charge without direction. Pistol shots cracked dully, mixed with the heavier boom of rifles. They shot at random, having no targets. When there was no return fire the rush petered out. They stopped and clustered—right in front of the barber shop, everybody talking at once. All of them had white cloths around both upper arms.

A thin hardacre, with a drooping black mustache, rode right up to the boardwalk and emptied his pistol into Shakey Burger's front window. Fargo could have reached out and touched the horse's foreleg. He eased the rifle back so it wouldn't be seen, crouched lower. If he fired from here, with them so close, they'd riddle him before he could get out through the narrow opening between the steps and the side of the building.

A Henry spat from somewhere up the road and one of the outlaws spun from the saddle. The others milled and another shot rang out. No one was hit.

"There! The livery stable. Come on!"

They rode off, shooting furiously. Fargo cursed aloud and squirmed out on the inside of the steps where the building covered him. What damn fool hadn't gone to the mine? He sprinted to the back, slid in the muck going around the corner. Firing came from the direction of Kunz's but he couldn't see what was happening from here.

There was a rickety stable flush against the backwall and Fargo clambered atop it, went from there to the streaming roof. It was flat, slanting slightly upward. Bending low, he moved to the front corner, raised his head and looked out. The horsemen were fanned out around the yard of the livery, pouring concentrated fire into the stable.

Then the shooting stopped, as if at a signal. Fargo raised his rifle and picked a target. Before he could squeeze off the shot the stable door lurched open, a man clinging to it for support.

"Hawkins!"

The miner was bad hit. He reeled into the clear, tried to raise the rifle. The outlaws fired as one man. And kept firing. Fargo triggered the Henry. A man went down. He forced himself to ignore the bullet-punctured body of the truculent young miner now lying still in the mud. He swung the rifle, snapped a shot and emptied another saddle. They saw the flash that time and two bullets whined past his head.

Someone shouted: "That roof!"

Fargo ducked. A rattle of shots sounded; slugs hit the flimsy false front, ripping through. He stood erect suddenly, searched for a target. Two horsemen were riding toward the building. He fired and saw one of them drop backward onto the rain-slicked roof. He rolled, came to his feet and ran to the back, vaulting out into blackness. He cleared the stable but he couldn't see the ground and hit hard, falling forward. The muzzle of the rifle buried itself in the soft ground.

He heard hoofbeats on wood and knew the other horseman had crossed the boardwalk and was coming around the side. He pulled himself up, leaving the useless rifle where it was, got his back against the building at the corner. His hands worked desperately at the mackinaw to get at the Navy Colt buttoned under it. There was mud on his hands and on the coat—his fingers couldn't get it opened! He caught a flash of a horse's head going by and then it was too late to pull the gun, too late for anything as the rider came into view and he was already swinging a rifle. He fired and missed, the bullet ripping a piece out of Fargo's hat-brim.

The man screamed a curse, jacking at his weapon. Fargo took a long stride, swung his leg in a vicious kick that landed in the horse's belly. The animal jumped and his rider shot again as he was falling from the gyrating horse's back. Fargo launched himself at the prone figure, landed full atop him. The rifle was pinned between them and Fargo got both hands on it. He laid the barrel across the man's throat and pushed. Eyes bulged and the bearded face contorted. Fargo put all his weight on the rifle and something gave with a nasty crackle. The man lay still, face up and staring with the rain pouring down.

He didn't feel it.

A gun slammed nearby and Fargo rolled instinctively, came up on his knees with the outlaw's rifle leveled. A dark figure on horseback had shot up at him from behind McCutcheon's store. He fired again. Fargo triggered the rifle, squeezing off three shots before the piece clicked empty. The rider hauled himself between the buildings as his horse dropped from under him.

No more than five minutes had elapsed since the attack began. Yet five Spoilers were dead, another unhorsed and Alva Hawkins would never learn how to shoot, now.

Fargo dropped the empty gun and started up the slope at a sliding trot heading for the upper town. That's where the other group had been headed, he was certain. And since he'd seen neither Hobie Spencer nor Charlie Ward, that's where they both had to be.

Hobie's group, with Charlie bringing up the rear, had pushed through the chill waters of the creek with the first gunshot from the lower end of town. Following the wide outlaw's white coat, they had crossed the road just below the smelter and made their way up the slope to where the houses of the miners began. Charlie urged his mount up beside Hobie as the leader stopped.

"Goddam, Hobie. These houses are all over the place."

They were, dotting the slope in helter-skelter fashion. No defined roads at all—only worn paths leading to the shacks and soddies.

Hobie was listening critically to the sporadic firing from below. His mustache was wet and bedraggled but the wide-spaced eyes showed no effects of his recent drunk.

"Sergeant, I don't like the sound of that down there. Not nearly enough action. We must speed up. You take three men—those three—and go down-canyon. Collect everybody you can from the shacks. We'll go up doing the same thing. Rendezvous at the jail quickly as possible."

He gathered the reins, waved at his four men standing soaked and miserable in the mud. After a dozen steps the night had hidden them. Charlie led his motley three to the nearest dwelling, a one-room soddie. Smoke curled up through the rain from a rough stone chimney at the back. He signalled and a man went to either side of the wooden door. The other planted a heavy boot against the planks and the door burst inward.

"Hurry up—get 'em out here."

Two of them dodged inside, guns ready. There was a curious silence. Then, one of them stuck his head out.

"Ain't a livin' soul in here, Ward. Nobody."

He rode ahead to the next shack, waited with drawn Colt while the door was broken down. Though light showed through the shutters, this house, too, was empty.

A chilling suspicion was growing in Charlie. All of the houses would be empty. He knew it. Somehow, Fargo—that sonofabitch Fargo!—had anticipated them, safeguarded the women and children. The three men looked up at him uneasily, ignoring the slashing rain.

One said: "Nobody in any o' these. What the hell we do now?"

"They got to be somewhere," Charlie said. "A whole town can't disappear. They—"

A flash caught his eye from a nearby shack—on the roof. He spurred toward the shack, straining to see through the gusts of raindrops. He pulled the horse to a stop, jumped quickly to his feet standing on the saddle. There was nothing on the roof. And nobody.

"Over here!" He dropped back into the saddle, nodded at the door as his men slogged up. A crude wooden sled leaned on the building. "Get on in there."

The door opened with the latch and two of his men slipped inside, guns ready. Charlie was suddenly conscious that he was hearing nothing but confused shouting from below. No sooner had the thought registered than gunfire erupted inside the shack. Pistol shots and then the deeper explosions of a Henry. He spun his mount away from the door, leveled the Colt. One of his men stumbled out, arms criss-crossed over his middle. He bent at the waist and Charlie saw dark blood gushing between the man's fingers.

"Fargo. . . ." he said, and pitched face-down in the remnants of slushy snow.

Charlie shouted to the third man, "Watch the door!"

He rode around the corner, headed the horse up the slight slope toward the back of the shanty. He reined the animal around the back corner and in one instant looked straight at eternity. Fargo, blackened face split by a mirthless grin, crouched under an open back window with a rifle leveled and cocked.

"Hello, Charlie."

And pulled the trigger. Charlie hauled desperately at the reins, lifting his horse's head. Fargo's bullet hit the animal between the eyes and it continued over backwards throwing Charlie and falling heavily. Dead. Charlie felt a bullet fan his ear and scrambled behind the horse as another shot sounded. He burrowed around the dead horse, hate rising in his throat like vomit. He fired over the flesh barricade. Four rifle shots, so rapidly squeezed off as to be almost a continuous roar, slammed lead into the dead animal. He could feel the shocks as the bullets hit. He lifted the pistol quickly and shot blindly in the direction of the window.

He ducked, waited; his chest burned inside like scald. He'd be damned if he'd lay and wait for it. He jumped up, swinging the Colt.

Fargo had gone. . . .

Chapter 16

HOBIE POUNDED UP as Charlie got back around to the front of the shack. The third man was gone, too. Hobie haunch-slid his mount to a halt, took in the dead man, Charlie's mud-covered clothes and shaken appearance.

"Fargo?"

Charlie nodded; he couldn't speak. Numbly he thumbed fresh loads into the Colt.

"What happened? I asked what happened, Sergeant."

Charlie rubbed a muddy hand over his face. "He was inside. Shot two of my men, almost got me. He's—"

"I know what he's doing, Ward. He's stalking us. He put the whole town underground and he's fighting us alone. What magnificent insolence." Hobie laughed, the broad face lifted. "An entirely worthy opponent, your friend Fargo. Are you all right?"

"I'm all right. My horse is dead."

"Listen to me, Sergeant. I've no intention of letting that gold get away. Go down below, bring J.T. and all the horsemen to the mine entrance. I'll take my men up there and we'll throw enough lead down that main tunnel to frighten those mice into submission." He shrugged. "At any rate, it's all we can do."

"But— Fargo. He'll be sniping at us. He'll pick us off one at a time."

Hobie's voice grew soft; he said, "Did you think this would be a church social? When I tell you to move, friend Charlie, it's best to do so."

Charlie nodded. "All right. I'll get Skeen and bring them to the mine."

Hobie gathered the reins in his good right hand. "You had three men. Where is the third?"

"I don't know. I left him here."

A scatter of shots came from the direction of the mine. Hobie spun his mount, sent him up the path at the best speed the ground would allow. The white coat was visible for a long way.

Left alone, Charlie crouched near the side wall of the shack. Get Skeen! The hell with that smooth-talking ape. Charlie knew Fargo and he had no intention of staying in the open. He would find a hole and wait for a chance. A good chance.

McCutcheon didn't dare breathe. He tightened his arm around Bugle where they lay under a locker, deep in the shadows of the store. A bunch of the outlaws had broken down the door and were ransacking the place. Their voices were loud and rough—yes, and afraid.

"Man can't fight shadows—goddam if he can, J.T. I'm stayin' right here 'til we see that signal light."

There was a bottle-on-glass sound.

"Go easy on that. One of you get to that back window, keep an eye out for Hobie's signal."

A pair of muddy boots thumped across the floor, stopped inches from McCutcheon's eyes. He tried to quiet the thudding of his heart, certain it could be heard so loud was it in his own ears. He closed his eyes and—for the first time since childhood—he prayed.

The interior of the jail was dark. Fargo's eyes, good as they were, had trouble seeing the expression of the man whose throat he held in one big hand. Eyes bulging. He released a little pressure and the man sucked air greedily. He was the third hardacre who'd been with Charlie Ward. Pale, thin-faced and scared to death.

"Please. . . ." the man croaked. "I told you the truth. Honest."

"You better had, badman." He listened for a moment. Firing up at the mine. He'd have to hurry. "Get up and light that lantern on the table. And don't do anything sudden—or that's the way you'll die."

"Yes, sir."

Fargo held the Colt in one hand, a Henry in the other, staying close to the hardacre while he lit the lantern. His hands shook so bad he almost couldn't do it. Light blossomed in the room and Fargo nudged the man.

"Step outside, hang the lantern on the hook to the right of the door."

The man walked to the door carrying the lantern as if it might explode. Fargo followed with the Colt pressed hard into the man's side. His boots squished wetly and he thought incongruously of Silesia's warm fire, Silesia's warm bed. Long time before that. If ever. Eight down and at least that many to go. Including Hobie, that crazy Indian and Charlie Ward.

"All right. Open the door and hang it."

The man did as he was told, a spatter of rain blowing in as the door was opened. Fargo jerked the man back inside, spun him.

"Get to the cell. Move!"

It was dark again inside and the outlaw bumped table and stove, impelled by Fargo's hand on his back. He felt his way inside the iron-strap cell and Fargo slashed the heavy rifle across his head. He fell and Fargo clicked the lock. He moved swiftly to the window, looked down-canyon. Water streamed on the glass obscuring vision. But he saw the five horsemen down by McCutcheon's, starting up the rough upper road to the jail.

Fargo stepped back so they wouldn't see him. He shoved the Colt into his waistband, buttoned the sopping mackinaw over it. That had almost got him killed already but he had to keep it dry. The five rode up to the front of the raised porch.

"Hey, Hobie! What's up?"

Fargo pushed open the door with a shoulder, took one long stride out and one to the side. Five open mouths and ten staring eyes. The thin one with the mean face had his gun ready. He fired hastily and Fargo killed him first. Another pistol roared. Fargo dropped to one knee, triggered the Henry as fast as he could rack it. Another man dropped and one slumped in the saddle but did not fall. He and the two remaining riders took off down-canyon, racing the terrified ponies headlong down the slope.

Fargo stood and sent a pair of shots over their heads. They wouldn't stop until the horses died under them. He smashed the lantern with the butt of the rifle. It had served its purpose.

The rain came down.

Silesia was worried about Burt Stapleton. The fool hadn't made it to the mine when the alarm sounded. She had been listening to the intermittent firing from the other side of the creek. As long as she heard gunshots, Fargo was all right. She had a serene confidence in his ability to stay alive. Damn fool Stapleton was another matter.

She and one of the miners were on watch in the main fall about thirty yards from the entrance. The others were farther back in a worked-out stope. She stood, gripped the rifle.

"Baldy, I'm gonna take a look for Burt. Don't go to shootin' when I come back."

The man nodded, squirted a brown-black stream of tobacco juice. Silesia walked quickly up the lamp-lit tunnel. Rifle held ready, she eased around one of the heavy timber supports of the entrance, slid to one side and stood still waiting for her eyes to adjust. Rain still falling. Gunshots from the mine, or thereabouts. They sounded harmless and spiteful dulled by distance and the pouring rain. She could see no movement, hear no activity on this side of the canyon. She started down the steep pitch toward Burt Stapleton's soddy.

She found him much closer than that. He was face down in a diminishing snow drift not twenty feet from the mine. The snow under his head was stained pink with rain-diluted blood and he was dead. She looked around, stock of the rifle tight against her hip. Then, with a toe under one shoulder, she turned the dead man over. The sight almost sickened her. Burt's head had been split from hairline to the bridge of his nose by the slim-bladed hatchet still imbedded in the wound.

Silesia shuddered. She turned and ran for the mine but she couldn't outspeed the chill breath of premonition following her all the way.

For the first time she was afraid for Fargo.

At that moment Fargo was stretched full length on the roof of the mine office, carefully unwrapping a wet slicker from a new Henry. Hobie Spencer and four men, all on foot, had the mine under constant pistol and rifle fire. Angling shots off the walls and ceiling, they just might get one of the mine's defenders with a ricochet. Bullets don't mind turning corners when there's nowhere else to go.

He poked the rifle cautiously over the edge of the roof. Hobie was out of sight, hidden by the wooden shed housing the steam mule. The other four were split, two on each side of the wide tunnel opening.

They were alternating pouring shots down the fall, Hobie calling orders and encouragement. One would dart to the opening, stand and fire four, five shots and then dash to the other side out of the line of fire from within.

Fargo sighted with care, waited until the next man moved to shoot. The outlaw fired two shots before Fargo's bullet ripped into him. The others were stunned—and not sure the tunnel defenders hadn't got in a lucky hit. A second man ran to his companion, bent to pull him away. Fargo dropped him on top of the other.

Hobie's big voice roared, "On top of the office! Get out of there—run!"

And they did. Fargo rolled over twice, came up standing three feet from where he had been. Three snap shots and both Spoilers were down in the streaming mud. Hobie had located him; a bullet sang by very close. He turned to sprint to the backedge of the roof and away. Before he could move, a heavy rifle boomed from halfway up the canyon wall and something hit the rifle in his hands knocking him backward off the roof.

He lay for a moment, stunned. A bullet whanged off a rusting ore car right beside him. He squirmed behind it, hands tingling from the impact of the heavy ball on the smashed rifle.

A reedy voice drifted down: "I got him, Hobie."

"Stay put, Turkey!" Hobie shouted. "He's alive. Keep him pinned."

The heavy gun boomed again and Fargo shrank back against the stone side of the mine office. The corner covered him at the moment. But the man on the hill could move and he'd be cold meat. Hobie had him for sure if he moved away from the ore car. If he didn't, the rifleman up there would find a better vantage and pot him like a broke-winged duck.

He got out the Colt, clumsy with his numbed hands. He raised up and fired at Hobie. A searing pain tore his ear and he flopped again. Hobie's slug had sliced the top of his right ear off.

The heavy rifle spoke again, deep-toned and deadly. The ball gouged a fist-sized chunk out of the stone at the corner. Then it came to him. That was a long rifle up there. It had to be loaded with cap and ball, a paper cartridge. He threw a shot at Hobie to keep him honest, and waited. Turkey's rifle bawled and Fargo was moving before the slug finished its ricochet.

He went around the corner right into the rifleman's field of fire but away from Hobie's. If he was wrong about that being a single-shot he'd never know what hit him. Then he was sprinting along the back of the building, turning the corner and running full tilt for the creek. Both guns banged behind him. He didn't miss a step.

Except the last one. The creek bank was glazed slick and he was going too fast. He hit the dark water flat on his back. The icy torrent caught him and tumbled him for what seemed a long time before he could pull himself out on the opposite bank. He lay face down and shivering, coughing up water. The Colt was gone.

The knowledge prodded him and he sat up, looking toward the mine. Couldn't see—too much rain-black night in between. But they couldn't see him either. He pushed his protesting body upright, started up the slope. There was a rifle at Silesia's.

At the cabin he debated going inside, resting a few moments. He was battle weary—almost numb with fatigue. But he couldn't stop. Not now. Charlie was still around and he wouldn't quit. Neither would Hobie. He walked to the stable, moving like a man on rails.

At the low entrance to the stable, he stopped. Something was wrong. His stomach rippled and he came alert. There was no sound. He bent his knees slowly, senses reaching. A blood smell, like a slaughterhouse. Another odor, rank and wild. He dropped to one knee obeying an instinct blindly.

There was a grunt from the dark and something smashed the doorway where his head had been. Then he knew who it was and surged up and in, grappling the smelly, slippery body of the Indian, No-britches. He got one hand around the writhing Indian, reached for eyeballs with the other. A guttural moan came from No-britches. Fargo pressed his advantage and then his foot hit something yielding on the floor. He fell, sprawling on the still-warm bodies of Billy Buck and Roger.

The knout whistled and he twisted desperately. The rock thunked sickeningly against one of the dead ponies. Fargo rolled. No-britches gave his dog yip, high and shuddery. Fargo's outflung hand touched a slicker, grabbed the rifle still leaning in the corner. There was time only to throw it and he did in time to stop a blow of the knout. His boots hit legs and he kicked out strongly. The Indian fell with him and they rolled in the filth and blood of the stable.

Fargo got hold of the rawhide of the knout, pulled it around the Indian's corded throat and drew tight. He stood, lifting the other by the leather that was choking him. No-britches surged like a scalded horse. Locked together they hit the flimsy wall of the stable, burst through into the rain-whipped yard.

He rolled in the mud. He'd lost the grip on the Indian's throat and he didn't have enough energy left to fight him off again. His muscles shook and he wasn't conscious of breathing at all. He got to one knee, fell forward and rolled over on his back, face to the driving rain.

No-britches yipped again, rising lithely from the ground. His hand pulled a throwing hatchet from his belt. He stood over Fargo, his victory howl rising. The arm went back, hatchet poised to throw. Fargo stared at death knowing there was nothing more he could do.

A shot rang out and No-britches stiffened. A jagged hole appeared magically in the smeared paint on the chest and the Indian sagged to the ground like boneless meat.

Silesia came from the mine entrance, her smoking rifle tight-gripped. Her face was pale and she searched his face anxiously.

"You all right? Are you?"

He nodded, too winded to speak. Together they got him erect and he leaned on her waiting for the return of strength.

"Hey, up there!" It was a reedy voice, high and thin. "I'm comin' up. Don't shoot or you'll be sorry."

Fargo took the rifle. Slowly, out of the dark, came a man in buckskins, soaked black, water dripping from thick braids. He carried a tall rifle.

"What do you want?"

The mountain man leaned on his long gun. "Got a message for you. From Hobie Spencer. Him and me and that army feller, we got Andy McCutcheon and his boy over there at the store. Hobie sez you come fer to parlay and come alone. Else we'll do them two some mischief. That's what Hobie said."

Turkey spat deliberately, turned his back on Fargo's rifle and strode down to the creek and out of sight.

Some nightmares never end. . . .

Chapter 17

"YOU BELIEVE HE'LL COME, Sergeant? It seems unlikely for a man so adept at survival."

Charlie Ward turned from the window where he'd been trying to see through the sheets of rain, watching for Fargo. He was drawn fine, his jaw muscles bulged and he started at every sound.

"I told you he'd come and he will!"

Hobie looked up from the pistol he was wiping. "Do

not shout at me, friend Charlie. Admittedly, you were the instrument of capturing those two." He nodded at Andrew McCutcheon and his boy, both standing huddled and white-faced behind the counter. "Yet I must say my respect for a man who has done what Fargo has is not lightly put aside. What sweet arrogance!"

Turkey Tom, standing quietly in the store's gloom, said: "He'd o' made a tail-twister in my time."

Charlie cursed, the praises for Fargo salting the green hate he carried. "We'll see. We'll see how the great Fargo takes a belly-full of lead! When he walks in that door he's a dead man! I'll make sure this time. I'll—"

He stopped, breathing heavily. He'd made a mistake —a bad one. Hobie Spencer stared coldly at him. Turkey Tom casually swung the long rifle cradled in his arms to cover him. Charlie took a big breath, tried to smile but his lips were stiff.

Hobie spoke softly, coldly: "I was right about you, Sergeant. I knew it." He spun the cylinder of his big pistol, thumbed back the hammer and pointed it at Charlie's chest. "Take his gun, Turkey. Friend Charlie has outlived his usefulness."

How could it still be night? Fargo stood on the boardwalk before Shakey Burger's smashed window and looked out at the rain. It seemed to him like hours and hours since the rain began—enough hours to bring another day. He felt dull, used up. His brain was packed in oatmeal. Andy Mac and the boy were in trouble. He had no illusions at all about what would become of them. Silesia stood beside him, sensing his mood.

"You've done enough. Let the others do this."

She didn't believe it; he could hear it in her voice. He touched a hand to the crusted top of his wounded ear. Gotched. Like a Missouri mule.

"No, Silesia. Surround the place, start shooting and they're dead. We'd get Hobie and the others, but—"

"You'll think of somethin'," she said. "Here they come."

Footsteps on the boardwalk from up-canyon. Then two hurrying figures became visible: Foster Prudhomme and the big, gray-haired miner, Murray. Bootheels on boardwalk. Fargo stirred and his natural awareness stabbed him. Bootheels. . . .

"I kept the others away—like you said," Prudhomme whispered. "Fargo, what can we do?"

Murray had an armload of weapons—two Henrys, the shotguns from the jail. Fargo straightened slowly. It might work. Against three ordinary men, it certainly would. But Hobie, Charlie and that wild-eyed old squawman weren't ordinary.

"Take 'em out of there, I guess." He grinned. "Me and Murray there, we both got big feet. Both those shotguns loaded?"

Murray nodded. "The double's loaded both sides. The other'n has one in the chamber. What's the matter with my feet?"

"We'll see. You three stay here. And stay back out of sight."

Weaponless, he walked to the top of the steps leading down the last level to McCutcheon's store. He leaned back out of range, peered around the corner. Light inside. But not much. Front window shuttered. They had no direct view of the steps and the boardwalk leading to the store. Straight out, they could see. But there was no window exposing this angle.

"Spencer!" His voice rolled and echoed. "Marshal Fargo. . . . I'm here."

The front door of the store cracked a hair. "Of course you are, sir. May I say it has been a pleasure fighting you—though unsuccessfully."

"Never mind the grease, Hobie. What's your idea? Why don't you throw down your guns and come out of there? That way you'll live to hang."

Hobie's rollicking laughter came, deep and full. "You're an arrogant man, Fargo. And I admit defeat.

But—not entirely. I'm afraid I must bet my two little deuces into your pat hand." His tone became businesslike. "You will listen. To insure the safety of the boy and his father, you must have prepared a load of gold. As much as one packhorse can carry. And mounts for all of us. We will release McCutcheon and the child on the far side of the rimrock. From there we shall take our chances."

"Not all of the gold?"

"I am an adaptable man, Mister Fargo. All of the gold was feasible when I had twenty men. Not now. One packhorse, as I said. And please believe the only other alternative is immediate death for these two—and as hard a fight as you'll ever have before you kill us. Your answer, please, in ten minutes."

The door closed.

Fargo moved quickly back to the others, rapping his heels heavily on the walk.

"It's going to work," he said. "Now, listen. Murray, when I go back to give him our answer, stay right with me. To the edge of the steps. When I say—'All right, Hobie, I'm coming—' *you* walk down the steps as if you were me. Walk slow and walk heavy. Understand?"

"Me?" The man's eyes shifted. "But I'm no—"

"They can't see up this way. Just walk slow and measured. By the time you get to the front door, it'll be all over—or at least there'll be enough ruckus so you can grab cover. All right?"

The miner looked from Prudhomme to Silesia. He swallowed heavily. "If you say so, Marshal. . . ."

Fargo took the two shotguns from him, checked the loads. He wouldn't need additional shells; three would be plenty or two-hundred wouldn't be enough.

"Foster, take those rifles from him. He has to be unarmed. All right, Murray—let's go."

They stopped at the top of the steps, Fargo gripping the two scatterguns.

"Hobie! Mayor Prudhomme says we'll accept—on one condition."

The door cracked slightly. "And that is?"

"I come in right now—alone with no weapons—and make sure McCutcheon and the boy are unharmed."

There was a short silence. Then Hobie said, "You are not a fool, Marshal. I know that. Therefore I must deduce that you have no idea of walking into a dark room against three expert guns with any thought of conflict. Come in. . . ."

Fargo took a breath, moved to the edge of the porch. "All right, Hobie—I'm coming."

He jumped soundlessly into the mud between the two buildings, started for the rear of the store. Behind him, he heard Murray's boot hit loudly on the first step.

Charlie Ward heard it too and something curdled inside him. "You damn fool, Hobie! You—"

The wide man whirled and his face was not pleasant. "Shut up! Get back against the bar!"

He backed, touched the wood and stopped. Dimly, he was aware of McCutcheon and the boy standing stiff and terrified behind the heavy plank counter. Footsteps on the boardwalk, slow and heavy. Fargo's footsteps. His eye turned to his Navy Colt atop a coil of rope where Turkey Tom had put it. Two steps away. Just two steps.

Turkey Tom, moving soundlessly, got to the far front corner of the cluttered room where he could cover the opening door. Hobie slid behind a stack of nail kegs, facing the door. The measured sounds of heels on wood came closer, got louder. They reached the door. And stopped.

Something, some nameless compulsion, made Charlie Ward turn his eyes to the rear of the long room. Fargo was there, stepping soundlessly into the room, one shotgun gripped in his left hand, another aimed over his left wrist in shooting position.

Charlie screamed: "Fargo!"

Turkey Tom reacted best and died first; he was still turning the long rifle when one barrel of the shotgun tore him apart. Hobie got around, snapped a shot and Fargo was hit. But he was already triggering the other barrel of the greener and the blast hit Hobie full in his wide chest.

Charlie shook his paralysis and grabbed the Colt. He vaulted the counter, chopping viciously at McCutcheon's head with the gun, diving out of sight and pulling the boy along with him.

Fargo leaned against the wall, pressing fingers to the hurt in his stomach. He'd felt the slug hit lowdown and he knew it was bad. He shook the weakness, made himself move behind a stack of mining equipment. There was still Charlie. Charlie, still hiding behind something. He had always found something to hide behind. Or someone.

"Come on out, Charlie. It's over. . . ."

He leveled the single-shot greener. There was a cry, a scuffle. And Charlie Ward rose slowly at the end of the long counter. Bugle McCutcheon was clutched to his chest. Charlie's eyes were wild.

"Why don't you shoot, Hero. Go ahead—shoot!"

He stepped into the aisle, raising his gun and Fargo ducked. The bullet hit a pitcher on a back shelf, shattering it.

Charlie shrilled, "I'm gonna kill you, Fargo! You know that? Finally I'll be rid of you."

Fargo steadied himself behind his cover; he'd have to keep the pain out of his voice, make it taunting.

"No you won't, Charlie. You'll funk out like always. Run like a castrated dog as you did at Wheeler's Hill!"

"You sonofabitch!"

It was almost a screech. He fired two shots, cursing incoherently.

Fargo laughed. And Charlie Ward broke again. He threw the boy aside, started down the aisle, firing as he came. Fargo summoned his remaining strength, jumped out in front of him, shotgun leveled. Charlie's Colt flashed and Fargo felt the shock of another bullet. His legs grew weak and he dropped to his knees, body still erect and the shotgun rock-steady. He pulled the trigger and blew a large and final hole in Charlie Ward. Then he folded forward over the gun, rolled slowly to the floor.

The rain had stopped and it was quiet in Gault. Very quiet. . . .

Chapter 18

MAJOR DEVOE WONDRUS came to Gault on the hottest day of the year. Heat shimmered in dust-caught waves in the airless canyon. The creek was a mere trickle. It was a working day but a surprising number of miners seemed to join the crowd at McCutcheon's store as the dapper army officer talked with Foster Prudhomme. For that matter it was a school day, yet every kid in town was there. Along with Silesia Bragg, Nellie Dempster—all three of the McCutcheons. Everybody.

It was a quiet, intent crowd and it seemed to make the major uneasy. "Mayor Prudhomme, could we conduct our business in a somewhat less populated place? That is—well, it is rather warm out here."

"You said to get several responsible citizens to sign those statements." Prudhomme shrugged. "They all want to."

"But it's—at least it's irregular. The judge advocate has an open file on Sergeant Fargo. We'd like to establish proof of death so we can close it."

Caroline McCutcheon said firmly, "He was a good man."

"Not to the army, Madam," the major said.

"He saved this here town," a burly miner offered.

"I'm aware of your feeling for this man. But he was a deserter in our eyes. Now—you have Fargo's sutler's card, his name-tag. It requires only four or five sworn statements attesting personal witness to the demise of this man. That's all."

The major mopped his streaming face. Prudhomme nodded. "All right. We just wanted it known how Gault regards the memory of the man who kept it alive. I was with him when he died. I'll sign."

"Fine." The crowd stirred and the major said hastily, "Not everyone. Understand—this is not to impugn the man's character. Only to establish his death so the case may be officially closed."

"I was there, too," Silesia said. "I'll sign."

Shakey Burger stepped forward. "I'm the barber. I buried him."

"Good. One more will be fine."

"Ja, me—I sign." Kunz pushed up to the others.

The major nodded. "Let's get it over with. I can't say I enjoy your weather."

In fifteen minutes it was done and the major rode gratefully out of Gault.

Silesia pushed slowly through the townspeople. Everybody seemed to be grinning, like at a secret joke. But there was nothing said. She was grinning inside herself and it moved to her lips as she joined him at the edge of the dispersing crowd. He was pale and still looked weak. The white streak in his hair stood out against the deep black of the rest of it. She took his arm.

" 'Most supper time."

He nodded. "Let's go home. . . ."